Kepler's
dream

JULIET BELL

Kepler's
dream

G. P. Putnam's sons

An Imprint of Penguin Group (USA) Inc.

G. P. PUTNAM'S SONS • A division of Penguin Young Readers Group.
Published by The Penguin Group.
Penguin Group (USA) Inc., 375 Hudson Street, New York, NY 10014, U.S.A.
Penguin Group (Canada), 90 Eglinton Avenue East, Suite 700, Toronto,
Ontario M4P 2Y3, Canada (a division of Pearson Penguin Canada Inc.).
Penguin Books Ltd, 80 Strand, London WC2R 0RL, England.
Penguin Ireland, 25 St. Stephen's Green, Dublin 2, Ireland (a division of Penguin Books Ltd.).
Penguin Group (Australia), 250 Camberwell Road, Camberwell, Victoria 3124,
Australia (a division of Pearson Australia Group Pty Ltd).
Penguin Books India Pvt Ltd, 11 Community Centre,
Panchsheel Park, New Delhi—110 017, India.
Penguin Group (NZ), 67 Apollo Drive, Rosedale, Auckland 0632,
New Zealand (a division of Pearson New Zealand Ltd).
Penguin Books (South Africa) (Pty) Ltd, 24 Sturdee Avenue,
Rosebank, Johannesburg 2196, South Africa.
Penguin Books Ltd, Registered Offices: 80 Strand, London WC2R 0RL, England.

PUBLISHER'S NOTE

Published simultaneously in Canada. Printed in the United States of America.
Design by Annie Ericsson. Text set in Kepler Std.

Library of Congress Cataloging-in-Publication Data
Bell, Juliet. Kepler's Dream / Juliet Bell. p. cm.
Summary: While her mother undergoes radical cancer treatment, eleven-year-old Ella stays with
her father's mother in Albuquerque, New Mexico, where she learns about grammar and family
history, and helps investigate the theft of an extremely rare book from her grandmother's library.
[1. Books and reading—Fiction. 2. Grandmothers—Fiction. 3. Swindlers and swindling—Fiction.
4. Family life—New Mexico—Fiction. 5. Cancer—Fiction. 6. Kepler, Johannes, 1571–1630.
Somnium—Fiction. 7. Albuquerque (N.M.)—Fiction. 8. Mystery and detective stories.] I. Title.
PZ7.B82432Kep 2012 [Fic]—dc23 2011024136

ISBN 978-0-399-25645-5

1 3 5 7 9 10 8 6 4 2

for Samuel and Romilly

and for Henry

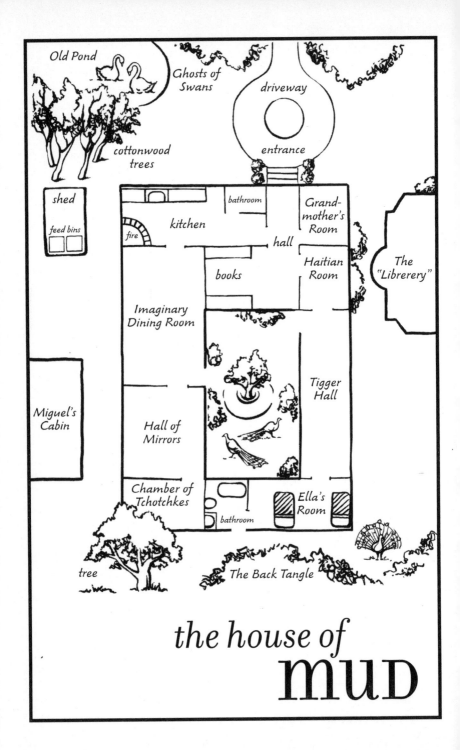

Old Pond

Ghosts of Swans

driveway

cottonwood trees

entrance

shed

feed bins

bathroom

kitchen

Grandmother's Room

fire

hall

Haitian Room

books

The "Librerery"

Imaginary Dining Room

Miguel's Cabin

Tigger Hall

Hall of Mirrors

Chamber of Tchotchkes

bathroom

Ella's Room

tree

The Back Tangle

the house of
MUD

contents

ONE

STAR LIGHT,
Star Bright

IT WAS THE MIDDLE OF THE NIGHT, AND THAT'S NOT A TIME when you want to be hearing strange noises. I don't care how brave you are. No one wants to be restless and almost-asleep, then rustled awake by a thudding overhead and the feeling that someone is trying to get into the room.

There was a tapping at the door. A whisper I could hardly hear.

"Ella!"

Someone was calling my name.

I sat up in the darkness. It was always so dark at my grand-mother's. I don't know what they do to the nights in Albuquerque, but whatever it is, it makes their midnight air thick and slippery like oil, and impossible to see through.

I listened.

I heard the scratching sound again, and then Lou started to growl. My dog Lou may have been softhearted, but he was as spooked by that house as I was, and if some ghost or monster really tried to get me, he'd want to protect me. The problem was, the rumble in his throat made it hard to hear what was going on. It seemed like an intruder was working away at the outside door to the bathroom. My bathroom had two doors, one into the room where I slept and one that connected to one of the murky areas behind the house, a scratchy tangle of brambly wilderness and rusty fencing and, for all I knew, buried treasure. I'd never been able to use that door to get outside. It was one of the features of my grandmother's house that seemed part of some mysterious, earlier time, when people were running around— actual children maybe. Not just ghosts.

"Ella!" I heard again. Lou gave a short woofle-bark, but I shushed him, saying it was OK. A breeze of relief cooled my nervous sweat: I recognized that voice.

"Rosie?" I whispered back.

"Yeah. Can you open the door? I'm freezing out here!"

That was the other thing about Albuquerque nights, even in the summer. They were *cold*. It was the end of June, but I always slept under about ten ancient, musty blankets, and even then, my nose, like a dog's, sometimes got cool and clammy.

"Just a minute." I kept whispering, because I really didn't want to wake up the GM (the name I had secretly given my grandmother Violet Von Stern). She had made it clear in some lecture or other—maybe the time she told me I must never go into her room without asking; or the time she said, with her trademark sarcasm, how *delightful* it would be if people could sound less like a herd of elephants stampeding through the hallways—well, anyway, it was clear that if I ever woke my grandmother up by mistake, I would regret it. I'd always been confused about the difference between corporal and capital punishment, but I was pretty sure the GM believed in both.

"Can you open the door?"

I could hear the shiver in Rosie's voice. I felt sorry for her, even though we weren't friends. I wasn't sure why. She seemed to think I was a wimp, especially since my embarrassing fall at the Circle C—which was too bad, because on the soccer field I'm not a wimp at all, I score goals and have "grit," according to Coach, but how could Rosie know that? We had met a few times by then, but it hadn't worked out. Just because you're both eleven doesn't mean you're going to get along. Friendship isn't a math equation. We might both have been stranded there that summer—me staying with my grandmother because of my mom's cancer treatment, and Rosie with her dad, who worked for the GM—but she and I didn't hang out.

Except, apparently, in the middle of the night.

Still, even if she hated me, I didn't want the kid to die of hypothermia. Besides, what was she doing outside my room? What made her wander away from her and Miguel's cabin at that icy midnight hour?

I was planning to ask her once I got the idiot door open, but the problem was, I couldn't. It had been frozen shut by years of neglect. There was no give in it whatsoever.

"I can't do it," I whispered to the voice behind the door. "I can't move the doorknob at all. It's stuck."

"I'm really c-*cold*." Rosie sounded miserable, and Lou

whimpered in sympathy. I wondered if she thought I wasn't really trying.

"Let me think for a minute here." But it was the middle of the night; I wasn't at my sharpest. I felt like Winnie the Pooh, tapping his head all stuffed with fluff. In real life I was pretty smart, my report cards were fine if you consider that important, but under pressure, some of that intelligence just leaks out like air from a balloon. Besides, thinking hadn't done much for me that summer so far. I had tried to think about my mom getting better, but she was still super-sick; I had visualized my dad coming out to rescue me from his mother's house, but he was off leading fishing trips and not planning to show up anytime soon; and I spent a lot of time imagining the end of July, when I could finally see Mom again, but it didn't seem to make the time pass any quicker. I was still stuck in New Mexico with a grouchy old lady, a hundred peacocks, and a girl who thought I was too pathetic to open a bathroom door.

"I'll come outside." What else could I do? I wasn't just going to say, *Sorry, Rosie, you figure it out, I'm going back to bed.* "Wait there, OK? I'll come and get you."

"OK." Rosie's voice sounded small and faint. This wasn't like her. I hadn't heard her talk much, but when I had, her voice was strong and confident. Something must really have rattled her. Maybe she wouldn't find me quite so useless if I saved her from death by frostbite.

But getting out of the house meant making my way in the darkness through all the rooms that were between me and the big chunky front door that clanged open or shut like the gates of a castle. The GM's home was an old adobe (I called it the House of Mud, but under my breath so she couldn't hear me) laid out in a rectangular shape around a small central courtyard where the birds and bugs hung out. The house itself was made up of dim, spooky chambers filled with junk or antiques, depending on how you looked at it. The bedroom I stayed in was at the back. Getting to the front door meant going through the long room with the armor and bottles and the tiger rug she called Tigger; the sickly yellow Haitian Room, currently occupied by Christopher Abercrombie, Our Honored Pest, I mean Guest; along the winding, cluttered corridor; and then by the bedroom of my grandmother herself, where she made potions or did voodoo or maybe just slept in her bed. Whatever she got up to in the middle of the night.

And I would have to do this whole journey in the pitch dark without waking up either the GM or her yappy dog Hildy, or for that matter Our Guest. Then go outside, clamber over old, falling-apart hen coops, past the *Librerery* with her thousand valuable books, through thornbushes, and around to the back, near my bedroom, to find Rosie.

Piece of cake! Or it would have been, if I had been half god or wizard or something. Unfortunately, I was a regular, mortal eleven-year-old, with ordinary powers.

Still, I made it. Maybe my dead grandfather's spirit was helping me along. I closed Lou in my room, telling him I'd be back soon, and then I got all the way through the house to the front door, tiptoeing as delicately as I could. I managed not to wake anyone up, as far as I knew.

Outside, the night air soaked me like a cold shower. I could hear stirrings and rustlings all around. It was probably just the birds, but in that light it seemed like there were snakes in the grass, and burglars on the roof, and creatures hiding in the Library waiting to reach out and grab me. The one good thing was that there were a zillion stars overhead. It was hard to believe anything too terrible could happen with all those constellations looking on.

"Star light, star bright," I said in a low breath, "first star I see tonight, I wish I may, I wish I might, have the wish I wish tonight."

I wished my mom would get better.

That was my regular, all-the-time wish. *Please let the transplant work. Don't let her die.* I prayed, thought, wished—everything. My mom had just had the stem cell transplant that morning. It was too soon to know whether it would save her life.

When I finally found Rosie, she was sitting huddled on a rusty old cooler-type thing on the back step near my bathroom door. She looked different, and it took me a minute to figure out why: usually she wore her hair pulled back, but now it was loose and tangly, like mine used to be when it was long. I had cut my hair short when Mom got sick, out of solidarity since she lost hers, and now it was in that awkward growing-out phase. One of the only good things so far about not being home in Santa Rosa that summer was that I could have all my bad-hair days miles away from the people I knew.

"Hi," I said, rubbing my arms in a useless effort to get warm.

"Hi." Rosie seemed shy all of a sudden.

"It's really cold out here."

"Yeah."

"So—" I said awkwardly. Well, someone had to start a conversation. We couldn't just sit there swapping small talk all night. "What's the matter? Why are you up?"

"I couldn't sleep."

"Oh." *And why are you telling me? Do I knock on your cabin door every time I can't sleep?*

"I don't know where my dad is," she added in a small voice.

"What do you mean?"

"I woke up and went in to talk to him, and he's gone."

"Gone?" I asked stupidly. The cold was attacking my brain cells. "You mean—you mean, he's just gone?" You would never know, at that moment, that I actually scored pretty high on comprehension tests at school.

"He was out earlier tonight, but he came back before I went to bed," Rosie explained. "And he didn't say anything about going out again. Usually he would tell me."

"Do you want to try to find him?"

Rosie looked at me like I was a moron. "Where?" she asked. "How?"

"I don't know." I looked up at the stars, like maybe the Big Dipper would tell me. If I had been Edward Mackenzie instead of Ella, it might have. My grandfather Edward, I had learned that summer, knew everything there was to know about the stars. He was an astronomer. I never met him. He died when my dad was a kid. Some kind of accident.

But being me and not Edward, I couldn't read anything up there. The stars blinked in the quiet and kept their secrets to themselves. "I'm super-cold," I mentioned.

"Come on. Let's go back to my dad's cabin." That seemed brilliant to me, so we wouldn't have to worry about waking up the GM. Plus I'd been curious to see Miguel's place. Unlike his daughter, Miguel had been friendly to me ever since the day two weeks before when he picked up Lou and me from the airport. He was one of the only bright spots in the whole setup. Still, I thought he might want to keep his home private.

"Are you sure your dad wouldn't mind?"

Rosie shrugged. "He's not here to mind. So tough luck for him." That was more the attitude I had heard from her before: no nonsense.

It was a short walk along a path Rosie knew well, past the feed shed and other strange storage areas. If the peacocks were bothered by us walking around in the night, they didn't make a racket about it. That was a relief.

The cabin was cozy after the stark cold of outside. A foldout couch that I guessed was Rosie's bed was made up with blankets and a pillow. In the corner I saw a shadowed cooking area, the kind of snug kitchen you get in an RV or on a boat. The place wasn't big—then again it wasn't filled with armor and tiger rugs, either. I liked it.

"Which is his room?" I asked, and Rosie took me to her dad's neat quarters. It had a small chest of drawers and an empty chair, a single, tidy bed, and a crucifix on the wall. I remembered talking once with this girl in my class, Jordan, whose parents were divorced—like mine were, like Rosie's were getting ready to be—about seeing where your dad lived. "Dad Pads," Jordan called them, and said they were usually messy and had lousy food. My dad's apartment in Spokane had been, the one time I'd seen it, a Dad Pad just like Jordan described. Ketchup, mayonnaise and beer in the fridge, clothes and gear every which way over the chairs. Miguel's place was different. It felt like a real home someone lived in, instead of some junky motel room that had gotten out of hand.

"See?" Rosie said in the emptiness. "He's not here."

I nodded. The only person in Miguel's room was Jesus on the cross, and he wasn't talking.

"The fire went out a while ago," she said, going back to the main room. "That's why it's so cold."

"Well, let's start a new one." I'd watched Miguel do it a hundred times in my grandmother's kitchen, so figured I could give it a try. I wanted to prove to Rosie I wasn't a complete good-for-nothing. I took a couple of big logs from the tin bucket, then Rosie scattered kindling over, then I added crumpled-up newspapers as a final topping. It was like making a sundae. Rosie found the matches and lit the edge of one of the papers, and away it went. Like a house on fire. Rosie high-fived me, her first real sign of friendliness, and then we sat on the floor, our backs against the couch, trying to get warm.

We got hypnotized, staring at the green, blue and orange flames moving around each other like in a dream. In a sort of trance I noticed two other doors in the farthest corner of the cabin. One was the bathroom, I guessed, but what was the other one?

I was about to ask her, when suddenly we both heard a loud, strange *bang*. Then another.

I thought it was fireworks at first. It wasn't the Fourth of July yet, but almost, and there are always those people who can't wait till the Fourth to get things exploding.

"That," said Rosie in a choked whisper, "sounds like a gun."

A gun?

But she was right. It hadn't been a *rat-a-tat-tat*, like fireworks: it had been two muffled cracks, like—well, like gunfire.

Rosie covered her mouth and pointed at a high shelf in the cabin. There was nothing there, so I didn't get what she was pointing at.

"My dad's rifle—it's usually up there. It's gone."

Now I was freezing again, and there was nothing the fire could do to keep me warm. We both strained to listen, but there was dead silence.

And then there was an incredibly loud wail that tore up the air.

It took a second to register that it was not the wail of a person but of a device. An alarm was going off like crazy, at my grandmother's house.

To me the cabin seemed a nice, safe place to be, and I wasn't eager to go anywhere else, but Rosie had a plan of her own.

"We've got to get out there. I have to find out if my dad is OK." This thin, tough kid, even if she wasn't my friend, was brave, too.

By the time we opened the door to peer out, lots was happening. Lights were on everywhere, birds were crying, and there were a hundred dogs barking, not just Lou and Hildy, but every other dog in a two-mile radius, it seemed. It was as if some big, ugly, middle-of-the-night party had just come alive.

"Come on," Rosie said urgently. Her hand clutched my arm tightly. "Let's see what's going on."

"OK," I said, like I thought that was a great idea, and off we went.

Outside, the scene was weirdly beautiful. It was like a stage, with these bright outdoor beams I'd never seen before lighting up all the peacocks, the feed bins, the cottonwood trees, and the House of Mud itself. It could have been a postcard picture: *Greetings from Albuquerque!* It was only the noise, and what it might mean, that made the scene a nightmare. Thieves? Murderers? Pirates?

I heard my grandmother and suddenly panicked that she had been hurt. What if someone had fired a gun at her? "Ella! *Ella!*" The high, scared voice hardly sounded like hers. "Where are you? ELLA!"

"Here! Grandmother—I'm here." Rosie and I jogged to the

front door, which was ajar. I slipped inside. Rosie let go of my arm and stayed outside.

There was Violet Von Stern in a long white nightgown, her skin like ash, her blue eyes fearful. She stood tall and upright, but her face was droopy and haunted.

At her feet, her dog Hildy (Brunhilda, for long) was yapping away and turning around in mad circles. Someone must have let Lou out of my bedroom, because he came and jumped up on me and gave me a big licky greeting.

"Ella," my grandmother said weakly, and reached her hands out. It was only the second time she had ever touched me. "Are you all right?"

"I'm fine, Grandmother. Are you?"

"What on earth is going on?" A gray-blond man in a purple bathrobe came out of the Haitian Room blinking, his eyes blood-shot. This was Abercrombie, Our Honored Guest. One of the last people I felt like seeing. "Violet, are you all right?" He didn't ask about me, I noticed.

"Christopher." My grandmother said his name as if to remind herself who he was. She was pulling herself back together. "There seems to be some sort of disturbance." A remark for the Department of Understatement, if you asked me.

The telephone rang in the kitchen, and my grandmother went to answer it. "Hello? Yes, this is Violet Von Stern." On the phone she repeated her remark about the disturbance. "Yes, you had better send someone around immediately. Thank you." She hung up. The alarm finally stopped.

I heard a scuffle outside. The front door opened again, and in came Miguel, his arm wrapped around Rosie.

"Mrs. V," he said in a hoarse voice. He looked spooked, too. "Are you all right?"

In his hands he held a rifle.

"Good heavens, Miguel," my grandmother replied, folding her arms across her nightgown. "Please, let me find a bathrobe. Wait there." She disappeared to her mysterious chamber. Tiny Hildy stood in the bedroom doorway looking important, guarding her mistress. She growled, which would have been funny under different circumstances. She was about half a foot tall. I tried to catch Miguel's eye, but he wasn't looking at me. Neither was Rosie.

"All right." My grandmother returned in a long golden robe and elegant flats, her hair brushed, lipstick on, even. She looked like a goddess, the kind you'd see on Halloween. "*We* are all accounted for, at least. Now—Miguel." She cleared her throat, *Ahem.* "Why are you holding that gun?"

He snapped the thing in two, as if it were a stick, so it hung broken-looking in his hands. "I saw someone out by the Library . . ." Miguel's voice was nervous. "I wasn't going to hurt them. I was just trying . . . trying to warn them."

My grandmother raised her eyebrows. *"And?"* she asked impatiently. "Did you see who it was? Or what the person was doing?"

He looked uncomfortable. "I'm not sure, Mrs. V. He—or they, there might have been more than one—got away."

"Maybe someone was trying to get into the Library," I piped up. "There's a lot of valuable stuff—I mean, *things*—in there."

Miguel gave me a strange look, as if I'd said something I shouldn't have.

"Kepler's *Dream*," Our Honored Pest said in a hushed, dramatic tone. He was talking about a book—the one that meant more to my grandmother, it sometimes seemed, than me and my dad put together.

"You're right." With an air of determination, the GM buttoned up her robe. "We had better take a look."

"Violet, do you really think that's wise?" Christopher Abercrombie asked. "Shouldn't you wait for the police?"

My grandmother dismissed the question with a wave of her jeweled hand. "Be good enough to accompany me there, Miguel, would you?"

"Sure, Mrs. V. Of course." He stroked Rosie's hair reassuringly and told her he'd be right back. Hildy trotted off with them, like that tiny animal was going to be a big help if they found a pack of burglars back there.

With just Rosie, Abercombie, Lou and me standing around, things got mighty quiet. And uncomfortable. If Our Guest hadn't been there, Rosie and I could have talked about what was going on, but as it was we were locked into silence, our eyes on the ground. Every second took an hour.

We heard footsteps outside the front door just as cars started to pull up in the driveway. The police were arriving. Miguel ushered my grandmother in and made a come-here gesture to

Rosie, who returned to the fold of his arms. My grandmother looked wide awake now, the General Major again. Her face was pale and fierce, her lipstick a bright, frowning line.

"Well," she said. "We can't know everything that might be missing right away, of course, out of the thousands of books in the Library. But one thing is clear."

She looked around with a stern, distressed expression. I couldn't tell from the way she was talking to us if we were supposed to be her soldiers, getting ready for battle—or if we were actually the enemy.

"Kepler's *Dream*," my grandmother said, in a voice heavy with upset, "is gone."

sunny
Skies

I HAVE TO BACKTRACK A MINUTE TO EXPLAIN.

It wasn't my idea to spend that summer at my grandmother's house. I hardly even knew my grandmother *had* a house—made out of mud or anything else. I'd heard that she and my dad didn't get along, and that she was maybe mean, or crazy, or both, but I had never met the woman before. She was like a made-up character, Cruella de Vil or Darth Vader, someone you've heard stories about but don't believe actually exists.

I should explain something about my family. When some people divorce, the situation is bad but not a complete disaster: people still see each other, or talk on the phone, or meet every now and then at a counselor's office with the plastic dinosaurs in the sandbox. The kids eventually get stepparents and maybe half siblings, back-and-forth schedules between houses and divided-up vacations. We had a lot of that in Santa Rosa.

But when we Mackenzies do things, we do them *all the way*. It's Extreme Divorce, like some kind of reality TV show.

So with my parents, the break happened when I was a tiny

baby. I guess one day they just looked up at each other and BOOM! realized they hated each other's guts—they must have forgotten to notice that when they got married. According to Mom, my dad "was never cut out for having kids," though there weren't "kids," there was just me, Ella. Anyway he ended up far away, like he'd been thrown off a moving train, in Spokane, Washington (say Spo-can, not Spo-cain), where he ran fishing expeditions in the wilderness. Fish seemed to suit him better than people. Maybe he felt bad about leaving my mom and me behind; then again, maybe he didn't. He sent the odd card, mailed guesstimate-type presents around Christmas (books for the wrong age group, toys mismatched to my tastes), and every now and then made his way down to California for a visit that involved some combination of bowling, ice cream and a movie, and embarrassed awkwardness all around. My dad wasn't a bad person—at least I didn't think so—he just didn't know how to be a dad. It was like no one ever gave him the manual. You got the feeling when our visits were over that part of him was thinking, *Phew! Got that* done. *Now, where'd my rod and reel go?*

So in Santa Rosa it was just Mom and me and Lou living together, happy as clams (who I guess are happy though I don't know why, when all they have to look forward to is one day being chowder). Or we had been until that winter of my fifth-grade year, when my mom got sick.

She had cancer. Leukemia. Leukemia sounds better than *cancer*, but as I learned from her doctor, the two words were too close for comfort. Leukemia, Dr. Lanner explained, was a kind of cancer, and it was in my mom's blood making her very sick. First, sick as in not feeling very well, hard to shake off that lingering cough, better get some tests done; then sick as in, Well, Ella, your mom has leukemia and has to start going to the hospital for chemotherapy treatments, and though they aren't going to make her feel great, the important thing is they'll help cure her; and finally, by May or so, sick as in, OK, no kidding, your mom has to stop working at her job, she has to be in the hospital all the time and we need a superhero, or a miracle, fast. Like I said, when we Mackenzies do things, we do them all the way. My mom had Extreme Cancer.

I loved Dr. Lanner, we both did, even when it seemed like we should hate him for giving us such bad news. He was tall and silver haired, with a kind, long face; he looked a little like Lou, actually, who probably has some bloodhound in him. He—Dr. Lanner, I mean, not Lou—nodded with a serious expression, like he was listening to you, but not too serious, like your mother was about to die and he didn't know how to tell you. He answered all my questions, even ones I realized later were stupid ("Can I catch it from her?") or that he didn't really know the answer to ("Is she going to be OK?"). The way he looked at my mother with his bright eyes, I sometimes used to get this fairy-tale story in my mind about them getting married after she got better.

But by that spring, when I was trying to finish up my science fair project—a cardboard construction I called the Consequence Machine where you started by rolling a marble that knocked down a domino and one thing led to another until at the end an Alka-Seltzer tablet fell into a glass of vinegar and there was a cool *fizz*—my mom's getting better was beginning to seem far away. On bad days, it seemed impossible. She had already had a boatload of chemotherapy, which turns you pale and bald as you probably know if you know anything about it. That hadn't done the trick.

So now Dr. Lanner was talking about a transplant operation—"stem cell," it was called, though what it had to do with stems I couldn't tell you. The idea was to zap all her old blood out and then pump her full again with better blood.

It sounded like science fiction to me (Wouldn't she die, in the part where they zapped her old blood? Would she turn into someone else, or an alien?), but this was real life and the only thing that might make her better. For the operation they planned to ship her up to a famous hospital in Seattle, where they'd lock her alone in a sparkly clean, antiseptic chamber for weeks, so no germs or bugs could get at her. "Sounds like Solitary Confinement," Mom said when he told her. Santa Rosa wasn't the best place for this—all the pros were in Washington, where they worked in between fishing trips, I guess.

Great plan. Let's save Amy Mackenzie's life. Oh, just one little problem.

Me.

Because anywhere other than in old-fashioned books, you can't actually have eleven-year-old kids living on their own in a boxcar, cooking on a gas stove and having adventures with their dog. I wouldn't have minded trying that—summer was hot in

Santa Rosa, and there was always take-out pizza if I couldn't find a stove. I had never seen a boxcar myself, though, and wouldn't necessarily recognize one if I did.

But in today's world, you have to place the almost-middle-schooler with some kind of house and grown-up. The first person we thought of was someone my mom called my "technical" aunt, her sister Miranda. My aunt and boy cousins lived in Arizona. We didn't really get along. It was like apples and oranges, or more like otters and elephants: two totally different species. When Mom and I talked it over, she joked, "Well, Ella, I don't want to say, over my dead body will you go stay with Miranda, because that seems like bad luck." My mom, as the nurses used to tell me in teary whispers, was famous for keeping her sense of humor throughout her ordeal. That's how you knew she was still Amy Mackenzie underneath it all. This (expletive deleted) disease might have taken her hair and her nice looks, but it hadn't taken her personality, in spite of its evil efforts.

(I should explain "expletive deleted." An expletive is a swear-word. I got the phrase from Mom, who used to say it instead of swearing. And *she* got it from Richard Nixon, who left the presidency in a cloud of shame and cusswords when Mom was a kid. Nixon, I guess, had a pretty dirty mouth—something he had in common with my dad—and when they wrote down what he used to say in meetings, they kept substituting "expletive deleted" for all the bad words. Like an earlier version of *bleep!*)

When the Miranda solution didn't work, because they were

going to Christian family camp in Florida, we weren't exactly heartbroken. We were still stuck, though.

The next obvious idea was to stay with Abbie. Abbie had been my best friend since first grade, and the Lunzes were a kind of substitute family when I needed one. They had helped us a lot through that spring, taking Mom to some of her chemo treatments or Lou out on a walk, organizing people to cook meals when Mom was too sick to manage. I went over there for sleepovers and homework afternoons with Abbie in their soft-pillowed den, where we snuck around on the Internet in between bouts of math sheets. I built my Consequence Machine over at their house, with Mr. Lunz giving me tips on construction.

The Lunzes were going to be gone, too, though, seeing grandparents in New York, and after that Abbie had sleepaway camp somewhere scenic. They felt bad, but had done so much already that you couldn't exactly blame them.

So there was nothing else for it. I had to find my dad. I mean, why have a dad if he couldn't take care of you in a situation like this? Even if he wasn't familiar with the contents of the dad manual, wouldn't it be obvious from plain common sense that this was a point where the guy ought to step up?

I was staying at Auntie Irene's by then, because Mom was in the hospital full-time. Irene Liu was our next-door neighbor, a super-nice person who seemed to assume from day one that it was her job under the circumstances to help take care of me.

Auntie Irene wasn't a blood relation—in Chinese culture you can call people aunts who aren't—but we were pretty short in the relations department, as you can tell. Irene would have taken me herself except that she worked eight-to-ten-hour days at the photo shop, and there's only so much time a kid can spend alone, whistling to a pet canary.

Irene helped me track down my dad. He wasn't big on e-mail, and leaving voice mail didn't get us anywhere, so finally Irene had the brilliant idea of contacting the outdoors company he worked for and pretending she was planning a fly-fishing trip for her nephew and had heard Walter Mackenzie was the best guide in the business. That got us a call back quick.

I don't think Dad was too thrilled when he figured out the trick. Auntie Irene's face was usually smooth and calm as a pebble, but her thin, pressed lips suggested that she did not think too highly of Walter Mackenzie as she listened to him talk after she explained our request to him. She shook her head and handed me the receiver.

"Belle, old girl! How are you?" came a surprisingly cheerful voice, as if my dad hadn't understood that I was not having the best of times. Still, he sounded friendly and was calling me Belle, his nickname for me. My heart went soft. The thing is, you want your dad to like you, even if—well, even if he's the kind of dad mine happened to be.

"OK," I said. "You know. Not great."

"Yeah. Listen, I'm sorry to hear your mother's not better yet.

That's crappy. But I bet those docs in Seattle will fix her up again. They know what they're doing up there."

"Mmm hmm." I wanted to believe what he was saying. I didn't want to imagine the other possibility. Me, Momless.

When he didn't add anything else, though, I finally had to ask. "And do you think, Dad, that while she's in the hospital . . ." *you could, you know—take care of me?*

My voice trailed off, and his became more businesslike. "Yeah, listen, Ella: here's the thing." And then he went on to explain that much as he would love to have me come stay with him *(Yeah, right, Dad!)* the problem was that now in May, and certainly in June, he just wouldn't be around, hardly, he'd be out guiding fly-fishing trips on the various rivers. He started to go into all this detail about Chinook salmon on the Skykomish and river trout on the Yakima, and he might as well have been speaking Eskimo for all that I was listening by then. The point was, he was saying No.

No!

I wondered what I had done to deserve all this: a sick mom, a flaky dad, a sure-to-be crummy summer. I must have gotten bad karma somehow, by cheating or hurting someone, but I had no memory of such a crime. Was it teasing Emily Holmes in kindergarten for pronouncing my name "Eya," something I still felt bad about because maybe she couldn't help it? Or the time I made Sierra Singer cry by saying she couldn't write for my and Abbie's second-grade newspaper, the *Mackenzie Lunz Tribune*?

Still, Auntie Irene must have had hidden persuasive powers. She shooed me out of the room so she could whisper fiercely for a few minutes with my dad, in private, and after that he came back on the line to talk to me, with a whole new plan.

His phone friendliness was more strained the second time around, but here is what he told me. My grandmother lived in Albuquerque, which was in New Mexico (*I know, Dad, we did state reports in fourth grade, Caitlin Berenson got New Mexico*), and although I'd never met her, she was a very—ahem—*interesting* person, and my dad was sure—or pretty sure—well, he was going to check, anyway—that she would be happy to have me. That she wouldn't mind having me. That it would be OK, for a while.

He reminded me of one of those ads on TV for some magical drug that is supposed to fix your life, but then under their breath they list all the things that could go wrong if you actually take it.

"Then maybe after the June floats are over, I can come out there for a visit, too. Though, you know, the Old Dragon and I don't . . . my mother and I don't always get along."

It was sounding better and better.

When I told Mom, I set up the news like this game she and I used to play together over dinner, before she got sick. (That seemed like the olden days now, back before cell phones and electricity, when dinosaurs still roamed the earth.)

We called it the Vacation Game. One of us would start by asking where the other one had gone on vacation, then that person would make up some fabulous tale about going to watch sheep shearing in New Zealand, or eating tasty crepes in Paris, or, like I once said, canoeing down the Amazon in Peru. Mom had had to stage whisper that the Amazon River didn't actually run through Peru, and so we settled on my having gone to the famous ruins at Machu Picchu instead. Which we then looked up online. I saw pictures of these amazing Inca buildings on top of a grassy, stony mountain in Peru, and learned that the whole place was like an incredibly early astronomy lab, where the Incas watched the movement of the stars and performed special rituals at the equinox. It all sounded very cool and like something out of a Tintin book. You had to go through jungle and rain forest to get there. I wanted to go there someday. For real.

"So," I said to my mom one day late in May, before I got promoted out of fifth grade. "Guess where I'm going on vacation while you're in Solitary Confinement?"

My mom was half curious, half out of it. She tried to act peppy, but she looked like someone whose batteries had run low. The light flickering off and back on again.

"I don't know, honey," she croaked. She used to say this disease had given her new sympathy for frogs. "Where?"

"My grandma's house."

She looked baffled. I think she was about to remind me that my grandma, the one I had known and actually called "Grandma," was dead, so I added, "Dad's mom, you know, who lives in Albuquerque."

"You're going to stay with Violet Von Stern?" She turned a paler shade of white. I hadn't realized she could go any paler.

"Yeah," I said. This was my grandmother, after all. What was she, a serial killer? Why should this be such a shock?

"Does your father know?"

Weird question. "Well, yeah—he was the one who called her. He said it was fine." (Actually what he said was "Mother promised me she wouldn't feed you to the birds." I think he was trying to be funny.)

"Violet Von Stern." My mother sighed, a heavy sigh with no humor in it at all. The plan seemed to alarm her, which didn't make me feel any cheerier about it, either. "Well. It will have to be all right." She was talking more to herself than to me. "Though the last time . . ." she muttered, and shook her head. "That *house* . . . All those *peacocks* . . ." I figured the chemo was making her ramble. Sometimes she would just stop making sense. All the chemicals they'd soaked her in—that stuff is bad for your brain.

The week between our deciding I was going to my grandmother's and my actually going to my grandmother's was a blur. I don't know how much astronomy you know, but from what I've read, when you get pulled closer to a black hole, time speeds up. That was what it felt like. For Mom, the black hole was the hospital room in Seattle; for me, the black hole was the house of Violet Von Stern. If I could have stopped time altogether and never had to go to my grandmother's at all, I would have.

Of course then I would have been trapped in fifth grade for the rest of my life, and I was just as glad to be done with that. After the ceremony for our "promotion" (I always thought that was a weird word, as if we were workers being told we'd done a good job and were going to move up in the world) everyone said good-bye, comparing all the different camps they were going to that summer: wilderness camp, soccer camp, music camp. I felt like saying, *Guess what! I get to go to Broken Family Camp!* but I wasn't sure anyone would get the joke. Our teacher Ms. Nelson gave me a special good-bye hug and told me I was a "brave, good girl," which made me feel like Lassie or a Saint Bernard. I had gotten a lot of sad, kind smiles from teachers at my school that spring because of Mom's cancer. I never knew what to do about it except smile back. I tried to look brave and good, though I didn't feel much like either.

The Lunzes gave me two great gifts before I left. From Mrs. Lunz, a pair of fancy cowboy boots. "It's horse country out there, you know, Ella," she told me. "You've got to be equipped." (I didn't know—Caitlin Berenson hadn't covered that.) And from Abbie, the best gift of all: she had the genius idea that I should take Lou along for the trip. "He'll be like your mascot," she said. This seemed completely inspired but also completely impossible, so when the word came back from my dad that my grandmother said it would be fine, I was amazed. "Mother likes animals," he said in his message.

It was the first positive thing anyone had mentioned about my grandmother.

Saying good-bye to Mom in the hospital that June is something I can still hardly think about. The scene is like the sun, in my memory—something you can't look at directly without going blind. I know I cried and she did too, though we were both trying to be brave and good. I hugged her as tightly as I could without suffocating her.

She explained how she was getting through this trip to Seattle and the transplant and everything by pretending she was going on a kind of special mission.

"This may sound a little crazy, El," she told me, "but I'm imagining I'm like an astronaut. I'll be in my airtight shuttle for a month and a half, going to some distant moon, where I'll pick up the cure for my leukemia. It's going to be tough and lonely, but when I get back, you know, the cancer will be gone, and life can go back to normal."

I nodded. The astronaut idea did seem a little crazy, but I liked the sound of going back to normal, after.

"Remember when you were little"—she touched my arm, and her touch was featherlight—"and we read all those books about the men who walked on the moon?"

I remembered. I was obsessed with the moon walk when I was in first grade or so. We studied space and the planets at school, and I decided I was going to work for NASA when I grew up. *The Eagle has landed!* I loved Mom telling me how she watched the moon landing when *she* was a tiny kid. It was one of her earliest memories.

"The super-famous guys were Neil Armstrong and Buzz Aldrin," Mom said. "But there was also Michael Collins. He was the one circling all by himself in outer space when Armstrong and Aldrin landed on the moon, in the Eagle. I always liked Michael

Collins. Not everyone knows his name, but they couldn't have completed the mission without him."

She paused. "Anyway, I'm sure he got scared. There were a thousand things that could have gone wrong for them: Armstrong and Aldrin could crash, the ship could run out of oxygen . . . Any of a million elements might have malfunctioned and they would all have died." She looked at me. "I'm sure Michael Collins got lonely. And missed his kids. They had to sit and watch the rocket lift off from Cape Canaveral just like everyone else, knowing their dad was in there and hoping that the astronauts would come back OK." My mom gave a watery smile, like she had finally gotten to the point. "And of course they did. The mission was a huge success."

"And they got to have a ticker-tape parade afterward," I added. I always liked those pictures of everyone waving from the car, with the confetti raining down.

"They did," Mom agreed. "They deserved it."

Then she promised that when the worst part of her treatment was over, I could come out to visit her. Looking forward to that day would help keep her going through the really tough part of the treatment. But for now, she had to buckle herself in and go.

"Now, Ella, sweetie, one more thing." She looked worn out, though. "I want you to do something for me while we're apart from each other."

I couldn't think about this too closely, the idea of not seeing her for almost two months. Not to mention the idea that she might never get out of Solitary. Ever.

"I'd like you to write to me," she said.

"Oh. You mean e-mails?" I nodded. "Sure. And I can send pictures, too. Auntie Irene got me a cool new cell phone—"

"No, Ellerby." This was my nickname when I was a little kid. She hadn't used it in a long time. "That's nice about the phone. But I'm talking about letters. Real letters."

"Letters?" I said weakly, like I didn't even know what she meant. Maybe I didn't deserve to get promoted out of fifth grade after all. "About—about what?"

"Anything. What happens to you—who you meet, what you see. Even"—she raised her hairless eyebrows—"about Violet Von Stern. Whatever you discover in her crazy house: buried treasure, dead bodies. Just write it all down, and let me know."

"Buried treasure?" That sounded better to me than dead bodies.

"It's possible." She winked. On purpose, I was pretty sure, though again with the chemo you couldn't always tell. "You don't have to do many, just even once a week would be enough. But I'll be counting on your letters to entertain me while I'm locked up."

The project sounded suspiciously like homework. But what was I going to do—refuse?

"OK, Mom," I told her. "I'll write you letters. I promise."

"That's my girl," she said, with that warm pride she used to have when I finished my book report, or scored a goal, or sent someone a thank-you note without her having to remind me a hundred times. It was the voice that told me I had done something good.

So, I don't know if you've ever been a kid flying alone. On the one hand, it's cool, because you're treated like royalty, with a special escort taking you to the front of the line and then onto the plane first, where you're handed over to some shiny flight attendant who greets you with a big, toothy smile.

On the other hand, you feel like an orphan.

I stared out the window while all the normal people got on board, and chewed my gum so hard my jaw ached. I sat and watched those guys out waving their orange wands around, trying to get the airplanes to sit, stay, or come, like instructors at obedience class.

To pass the time I fooled around with my phone. I squinted when I saw how hideous my short hair was in the graduation pictures with Abbie and me. Then there were a few of Mom in the hospital wearing this knitted cap someone had given her to keep her bare head warm. It might have made a nice tea cozy, but on her head it made her look like one of those people who stands in the shopping plaza handing out pamphlets about God.

"Sweetie, it's time to turn that off now." A Sunny Skies flight attendant with a badge that said KRISTY suddenly hovered over me. Her voice was kind, though—she didn't sound saccharine-fake, like they sometimes do. "Is this your first time flying alone?"

I nodded. I didn't want to be a baby about it. *It's just that my mom has cancer!* I felt like saying, but it seemed inappropriate.

"Well, it should be a smooth flight. And if you need anything at all, you just let me know. Who's meeting you at the other end?"

Some guy I've never met before in my life, who supposedly knows my dad. Miguel Aguilar was, according to my dad, a good guy who worked for my grandmother and had a daughter "around my age." Given how spacey Dad was on specifics, though, I figured the kid could be anywhere from five to fifteen.

"I'm going to visit my grandmother," I told Kristy, to keep it simple.

"Oh, how nice!" Her face brightened. "I'm sure she'll be glad to see you."

Actually I think she was pretty much forced into the arrangement. We both were.

"Listen, I've got to do the safety announcement now," Kristy whispered, putting a hand on my shoulder. "But later, I'll check in to see how you're doing."

So she went through the famous mime about the sudden loss of cabin pressure and oxygen in the ceiling, the life vest that would save you and the small tube to blow in if you started to deflate. I wanted to steal one to take with me to Violet Von Stern's.

The sunny skies themselves were fine, though, once we were flying around in them. I put my headset on so my iPod could wash any thoughts out of my brain, drank a cola, normally against the law in our house, and had a few handfuls of salty peanuts. Kristy kept her word and checked in on me a few times.

I always gave her a peanutty smile, like it was no big deal, what was I, a fifth-grader still? No, I was not, soon I'd be in middle school and flying by myself was a breeze.

When I came out, there was a tall man in a blue shirt and cream-colored cowboy hat standing near the gate barrier, with a tag on that said MEETING ELLA MACKENZIE. He had kind eyes and walnut skin, and when he introduced himself as Miguel Aguilar, I knew right away that he was a good guy. My dad had been right about that, at least.

"I know you have a travel buddy for us to find, too," Miguel said as we walked through the airport, which in New Mexico they call a Sunport. So we went to the baggage claim area, where eventually Lou was led out on a leash by some handler and we had a movie-like reunion, with him jumping up and licking me all over.

The whole day kept unspooling like a movie. Outside, the air was hot and bright like the desert, and there was a pink-colored range of mountains in the distance. When Miguel saw me looking at them, he smiled and said, "Say hello to the Sandias," as if he were a host and those mountains were part of his family. By then I was climbing up into a huge red pickup truck with Lou and feeling like this was the only way to travel. I half hoped that we would never have to get to my grandmother's house at all.

"You look like Mrs. Von Stern," Miguel said, glancing sideways at me as we started jouncing away in the truck. "Do people say that to you a lot?"

"Not so much." My mom used to tell me every now and then

that I looked like my dad—but in a tone that made it clear that it would have been better if I didn't.

So then Miguel asked how Dad was doing, and I gave my standard Dad speech about his fishing trips. Miguel asked about my mom, too, and I gave my standard Mom speech about cancer. And just when I was pretty much all speeched out, we rattled off the highway at an unpromising exit, passing some gray buildings behind high barbed-wire fences with signs that said WARNING: ELECTRIFIED FENCE. KEEP OUT. I saw a sign on the fence that said Juvenile Correctional Facility.

"So," Miguel asked me, like these surroundings were perfectly normal. "How long's it been since you've seen your grandmother?"

"Never," I answered. "I've never met my grandmother before."

"Really?" He frowned, and shook his head slightly.

I wondered if maybe Miguel didn't know quite what a weird family we were, all far apart and not talking to each other, but before I could think more about that, the truck suddenly took a sharp turn off a nothing-in-particular stretch of road into a hidden dusty drive. You'd never know there was a driveway at all—there were no other houses on the street we'd left, just weird industrial buildings and that big ugly fenced area.

The truck shuddered to a stop on the gravel, under a high canopy of trees. Around us were tangles of bushes and a scurry of creatures running here and there, followed by a huge *thump* overhead. I jumped. Lou barked. Suddenly it seemed like we were on safari and some lion or an antelope had just landed on top of the truck.

"Don't worry, that's just a peacock," Miguel said with a laugh. I saw a blur of brilliant color by my window. "There are a lot of them around. You'll get used to 'em. They don't hurt anyone, they just make a lot of noise."

I looked through the window and saw that we were surrounded by birds. Dozens and dozens of them, with their beautiful blue necks and topknots and green, fanning tails—and the less fancy brown ones, who were the girls, of course. Lou and I stared. I had never seen so many peacocks in my life.

"How many are there?" I asked.

Miguel shrugged. "Nobody really knows. Eighty? A hundred? It's not like they'll line up so anyone can count 'em."

Gradually I got that animal feeling that there were eyes watching us, too. At a short distance from the truck, waiting in the turquoise-painted doorway of a low, dirt-colored building, stood a tall, white-haired figure in an emerald-green dress. She was holding something in her arms, I couldn't see what.

I felt glued to my seat. At that moment I never wanted to leave this truck, ever.

Miguel took off his sunglasses so I could see his eyes. "Come on, Ella," he said gently. "Come say hi to your grandmother. She's excited to have you here for a visit." He looked back toward the lady and gave her a reassuring wave. "But," he added in a low voice, "you might not be able to tell that right at first."

I swallowed and hopped out, and got ready to meet Mrs. Violet Von Stern.

THREE

THE GOOD GRAMMAR
Correctional Facility

MY GRANDMOTHER STOOD VERY STRAIGHT. SHE WAS TALLER than I had imagined, with jewels around her ears and neck so bright, she glittered. Her eyes were as blue as the necks of the peacocks, her mouth a lipsticked red. She had the air of a queen. She was smiling, sort of, as she watched me approach.

She looked exactly like my dad—if Dad were an old lady with white hair and an emerald-colored dress. It was eerie. She was more Dad than dragon.

"Hello, Ella," she said from the doorway.

She didn't seem to want to move, and I wasn't sure what the procedure was here. Was I supposed to go hug her? Shake her hand? Curtsy?

"Well! You're dressed for ranch work, I see," she said.

My heart started to pound. Over blue jeans I had on my Bernie's Burgers and Dogs T-shirt. Mom had brought it back from Chicago when she was there for an optometry conference, and I had worn it for good luck. Suddenly it seemed clear that I should have been in an outfit suitable for a concert, or promotion. At the very least, a nice shirt.

"My other clothes are all packed," I stammered. "Sorry." *No one told me there was a dress code! Don't tell me I'm going to have to wear skirts all summer.* "I'm glad to see you—uh—Grandmother."

I felt like I was speaking a part in some out-of-date play. Who in the world calls their grandmother "Grandmother"? But "Grandma" didn't seem to fit. Dad had suggested "Grandmother" to me on the phone, and judging from her nod, he got that right.

"You like to wear your hair cropped like that, do you?" she added, with a skeptical look at the hatchet job on top of my head. "Is that the fashion in Santa Rosa?"

I shrug-nodded. In the cancer wards, it was. But I wasn't about to go into an explanation of all that now.

As I got closer, the object in my grandmother's arms started yapping. It was a high, grating sound, and I almost jumped out of my flip-flops. I had no idea the furry thing in her arms was *alive*.

"Oh, don't be ridiculous, Hildy," she said, scratching what I could now see was the head of a tiny animal. "There's no need to be jealous. This is Brunhilda. Named for the German warrior. Where's yours?"

"My what?" I didn't have a German warrior. Was I supposed to pack one of those, too? Why hadn't someone sent me a list?

"Your *dog*." My grandmother's voice dripped with impatience.

"Oh. He's in the truck," I said. "I think the peacocks—you know—scared him."

"The birds? Piffle! They won't hurt anyone. Why don't you let him out? Introduce him."

This did seem like a good idea—like the knight going to get his special, magical sword that protects him against the Forces of Darkness. Lou was the only one on my side at this point. Miguel, after carrying my bags into the house, had disappeared.

So I got Lou down and told him he was a good boy, and of course the first thing he did was run around and pee against a flowerpot near the house, which got Hildy yapping again. (I was going to stick with calling her Hildy. I couldn't call a dog that size *Brunhilda*.) I thought that we might both be arrested for defacing the property, but my grandmother didn't seem to mind.

"What's his name?" She looked down from her great height, her face a bit softer. "Some kind of hound, is he?"

"Lou," I answered. "He was a rescue dog, so we're not sure, but he seems to have some Lab, maybe mixed with bloodhound."

Hildy was still yapping so my grandmother said, "Hush, Brunhilda!" sternly. "This is Lou, and he will be your guest for the next month or two, so you're going to have to learn to get along." She let Hildy out of her arms so the two dogs could do their dog thing together, sniffing and circling and checking each other out.

"Lou will get used to the peacocks," she assured me. "Everyone does, after a while." There were maybe twenty birds wandering around on the ground near us, and four or five pacing along the roof above her head, looking nervous, like people waiting for a dentist appointment. A few others called out from the tops of the trees—a high, sad sound, like grief.

"Come in, Ella," my grandmother said at last. "Let me show you where you'll be staying." She opened the screen door, and in I went to the House of Mud.

We came in to a dim, cool entryway. In the clutter I saw a tall umbrella stand holding a bouquet of peacock feathers; a metal tin the size of a barrel filled with cashew nuts; heaps of magazines on the floor; a broad table crowded with stone creatures (polar bears, penguins, seals); and two white wicker chairs that faced each other across a kind of gangway. Straight ahead was a wide screen that gave out onto a courtyard with flower bushes, more birds and one pretty, silver-barked tree. Around the corner was a packed bookcase, with every kind of magazine and catalog scattered across its top.

"I hope you don't mind a few papers and books here and there," my grandmother said—which was like Niagara Falls asking if you minded getting sprayed by a drop or two of water. "I like to read."

I nodded. "Me too."

"Good." A positive word from Mrs. Von Stern, at last! "This way," she called over her shoulder like an expedition leader. She opened the door into a dark, cavelike chamber. "We go through the Haitian Room first."

It was hard for my eyes to adjust in the Haitian Room, as the only light came from a tiny half-curtained window, but eventually I could see acid-yellow walls almost entirely covered by colorful paintings: of beaches and marketplaces, cars and mopeds, wagons piled high with fruit. Hanging separately, in the corner, was a pencil drawing of a cute, round-eyed little boy.

"I've collected these paintings from various travels over the years," my grandmother explained in a bored tone. "And that"—she waved at the penciled boy—"is Walter, of course."

I stared. I would never have recognized that kid as my dad. I had hardly ever thought about him being a kid; it was hard enough to get a handle on him as a grown-up. No one ever got the idea to show me pictures of young "Walter." I had seen photos of Mom, in albums at the house of my other grandma, in Los Angeles—the one who really *was* a grandma, when she was alive, the kind who sent Christmas presents and baked brownies. My favorite picture from one of those albums was of small, blond Amy at a table with kids and balloons—black and white balloons, it was an old photo—and a huge birthday cake with seven lit candles. She was leaning in, her lips getting ready to blow.

"Ella!" my grandmother called sharply. "Must you dawdle?"

I hurried out of there.

Lou was trotting ahead. He and Grandmother (I still felt weird calling her that, even in my head) had gone out through a different door into the next room, which seemed like a great hall. The more of the house I saw, the smaller I felt. Was I somehow shrinking? There was no furniture in this room. I mean nothing regular like a couch or a rocking chair. Still, it was absolutely packed with . . . STUFF. Racks of bottles, wine, I guess, or maybe potions; a suit of armor; two mini–totem poles; another overflowing bookcase; and everywhere more paintings, of ships, giraffes, lakes, mountains. Across the floor lay a flattened animal with a fierce dead head that made the hackles go up on Lou's back. Mine too. It looked like roadkill—if you lived in India, maybe.

"That's my tiger skin," said our tour guide proudly. "I call him Tigger. Sweet, isn't he?"

Not really. Had she killed the animal herself? It wouldn't have amazed me.

"Now, this"—my grandmother walked down a few steps at the end of the hall and ducked her head under another doorway—"will be the room you and Lou share."

After the rest, it was surprisingly normal: a regular size, with two twin beds and a table between them. The kind of room you might find in an actual home, rather than a place that was a cross between a museum, a junk shop, and the set for a horror movie.

One difference was the real daylight inside there. Along the near wall were windows that looked out onto the courtyard. Eventually I figured out that the House of Mud was built in the shape of a rectangle with the courtyard in the center, though you couldn't do the entire circuit because there was a dead-end at my bedroom. But you could walk from my room all the way around and end up in yet another dark and dusty chamber, filled with papers, photographs, mouse droppings, and masks from Africa.

I needed a map.

"Here is a list of people who have stayed in this room." Grandmother pointed to a stretch of wall by the doorway, thirty or so names going down, pen or pencil scribbles on white paint. I saw my dad's a couple of times, and next to it once . . . my mom's. That made me shiver. Those were two names, *Walter and Amy Mackenzie,* I never thought of in the same breath. They didn't belong side by side. "You may add yours when you leave," she added. Sure, if I ever got out of there. "A pen is on the writing desk, where you'll find stationery as well."

Another part of the conspiracy to get me to write letters.

"Well, Ella." My grandmother cleared her throat. "I'll let you take a rest and freshen up after your journey. Dinner will be early—five thirty. You can come out to the patio at five, if you like, for iced tea. I imagine you'll want"—she gave my outfit another skeptical look—"to put on some different clothes."

"OK." I should have packed a ball gown! I knew there was something I was forgetting. "Thank you." I remembered to say that, at least.

"I hope you'll feel welcome," she said before leaving my cell, I mean bedroom, but as she was practically in Tigger Hall when she said it, I wasn't even sure I had heard her correctly. *Welcome?*

"Well, Lou," I said to him quietly, when I was sure she was

gone. "I've a feeling we're not in Santa Rosa anymore." He didn't get the joke, though.

Filling the time between "I hope you'll feel welcome" and five o'clock was a challenge. I sent a few notes on my phone to Abbie; told Lou to stop drinking water from the toilet, a bad habit of his; and found a spider that looked like a tarantula, caught it under a cup, and left it near the outside door, which I tried but couldn't open. (No escape there.) I spent a while looking at my face in the blurry bathroom mirror: blue eyes, straight nose and my "cropped" brown hair—my grandmother's word made me feel like a dog sent to a crummy groomer. I tried to figure out if I really did resemble this lady who was (reluctantly) letting me stay in her house. I could only sort of see it.

Finally I took a shower. Standing in the brown-stained tub, I tried to tell myself things could be worse.

It took me a minute to figure out how, though.

Then I came up with it: I could be stranded a million miles away from my mom who had cancer, staying with an old dragon of a grandmother who didn't have any Internet connection or TV—AND there could be no running water.

That would have been worse.

On the dot of five o'clock I set out on my return journey to the main entranceway. I wondered whether I should write my will before setting off in case I never made it. *(To Abbie, my autographed Giants baseball; to Auntie Irene, my authentic Bionic Woman Barbie; to Lou, my secret stash of beef jerky ...)* The Haitian Room was a little scary, because the place was dark as a grave, but I asked the penciled face of my dad to help us through, even if I couldn't see him, and I guess that worked. When we got out to the stone polar bears on the table again, I almost waved at them in relief.

My grandmother emerged from another door, now dressed in ruby red. She came out in such a way that I couldn't even catch a glimpse of her bedroom back there. This made me wonder if that was where the buried treasure was—or dead bodies, possibly.

"Ah! You've changed," she said approvingly. I was wearing a cotton flowered shirt and a long skirt that made me feel girly, which I usually don't, much. It was the closest thing I had to a gown. She said hello to Lou politely, and then helped me take him out into the courtyard where he could "relieve himself." Tucked over by that screen door I saw a few other low bookshelves that I hadn't noticed before. It was like the house was breaking out in a rash of books all over.

"Now," Grandmother asked, once Lou was out there meeting and greeting a few of the peacocks, "do you take iced tea?"

"Um . . ." I stood stupidly, trying to figure out whether she meant had I stolen any, or did I want to take some back to my room, or what. "I, um—"

"I've always wondered," she interrupted, in the tone of someone who has just found gum on their shoe, "why people say *um* rather than simply not speaking. It's such an ugly syllable." She crossed to yet another door, disappeared for a moment, then returned holding two tall, filled glasses. "I took your *um* as a yes." She handed me one.

"Thank you." It was around now that I started to think of my grandmother as a general major—the GM. I half wanted to salute her.

We sat on the wicker chairs, sipping our iced teas. There was an uncomfortable silence. I am often pretty chatty, but I couldn't think of a single thing to say.

"Your father tells me," the GM said eventually, "that you like to play soccer."

"Yeah."

"Do you mean yes?"

"Y-*yes*." I cleared my throat. "I'm on a team called the Hawks."

"Hawks?" She raised an eyebrow. "We used to have a pair of hawks that nested in the cottonwood trees. Then one morning, completely unprovoked, one swooped down and attacked a sweet little dove I kept as a pet. The hawk tore it to pieces, right in front of its mate, which died of shock a few days later."

"Oh. I—"

"So I've never been terribly fond of hawks since then." The GM took a sip. "Actually, I had Miguel shoot that bird, I was so mad at it." She sounded slightly guilty. "And he did, too. Got him with one bullet. So don't ever cross Miguel, that's my advice. He's a good shot."

She wasn't exactly smiling as she said this, but I figured it had to be a joke. Didn't it?

"Tell me, Ella. Do you like to fish?"

"What?"

"'*Pardon?*'"

Oh (expletive deleted)! "Pardon?" I repeated, like a parrot.

"Do you like to fish?"

"No." It is possible that some small attitude was beginning to leak through in my voice. The General Major was wearing down my manners. "Why?" I said. "Do you?"

"Heavens, no." Again, the raised eyebrow. "Can you imagine me sitting on a grassy riverbank, pole in hand, waiting for the telltale dip of the line?"

I had to admit that I couldn't.

"But your father likes to fish." Oh, so this was what she was getting at. In spite of the penciled boy in the other room, I kept forgetting that my dad was the GM's son. It seemed so improbable—like Cleopatra turning out to be the mother of Davy Crockett. Also, she talked about him as though he were some distant cousin. Not her own offspring.

"Has Walter ever taken you with him?" she asked. "—Fishing?"

"Once." I wondered if she even realized how often I saw my dad, namely hardly ever. She did know I didn't live in Spokane, didn't she? And that my mother had cancer? So far she hadn't said a single word about it.

"One time, Dad came to California for a visit." *To California, where I live with my mom, you know?* "He wanted to take me on an early-morning fishing trip. So he came by our house at, like, four in the morning . . ."

"Ahem!" she said. "Was it *'like'* four in the morning, or was it actually four in the morning?"

I blinked. "It *was* four in the morning." I decided not to fight the grammar police. It was more fun to remember the story. "Anyway, he said it was easier to catch the fish when they were still dreaming and not awake yet. So we drove somewhere way up the coast, and got there before it was even light out yet. But there was a diner open and Dad said we should have breakfast. I wasn't hungry at all, but he made me eat this huge breakfast, and then we got onto a small boat, with a rod and reel and a bucket of bait—"

I looked up. She seemed interested, amazingly, so I kept going.

"So we loaded up all the gear onto the boat and got on with a few other guys. But when the boat went out onto the waves, it got pretty choppy—"

"Oh, Ella. Don't tell me you lost your breakfast."

"No, no. I got to keep the breakfast."

She snorted, a sound that was maybe supposed to be a laugh.

"But I did feel queasy standing up on the deck, so Dad said he'd watch my pole if I wanted to lay down—"

"Lie down," she corrected.

"*Lie* down, and so I did, and I fell asleep, and I slept through pretty much the whole expedition and woke up when we were pulling back in to the harbor."

"Well!" Grandmother looked strange. It took me a minute to understand why. She was smiling, that's why. "I think that shows excellent judgment on your part."

A compliment! That was a first. "And after that, as a joke, Dad liked to say I was this great fisherwoman, because practically no fish bit on his line all morning, but he caught four bass and a couple of snappers on mine. He gave one to my mom to cook for dinner."

"Quite right." My grandmother nodded. "Speaking of dinner, shall we eat?"

Still not a word about my mom. I was beginning to get annoyed. On the other hand, I was also starving.

I followed her through the door that faced the entrance to her bedroom, and into another long, dim room, divided in two: the first half was a kitchen, the second half tables and clutter. There was one small round table in there, set for dinner, near a large raised fireplace with a fire roaring away inside it. (Evenings came on fast and cool there.) Along the side wall was another surface completely covered—I was getting used to this—with letters, magazines, photographs, money, stamps, marbles in a silver dish, glasses, pens, a few books, and a long cylinder that was either a spyglass or a stick of dynamite.

"You sure have a lot of—" I started, but she cut me off.

"I have a lot of things, I know." My grandmother's voice was brisk. "I implore you, never call it *stuff*. I can't bear it when people come into my house and say, 'Goodness, Mrs. Von Stern, what a lot of stuff you have!'"

Another thing to remember. I'd have to make a list.

"I collect. I am a collector, and I travel, and so after a time"— she shrugged—"objects accumulate."

This was what Ms. Nelson would have called an understatement. She made us write a whole page of understatements once.

I enjoyed that. *I have a slight dislike for anchovies. My dog isn't very clean after a walk in the rain. I might prefer it if my mother spent less time in the hospital.*

Dinner that first night was edible. No anchovies, at least. Hildy sat right at my grandmother's knee and got bites of roast beef handed to her from the table, though we had fed both dogs before we sat down. The best thing about the meal was dessert: a delicious chocolate cake with raspberry cream frosting. My grandmother apparently had a sweet tooth—something we had in common. Maybe it was genetic.

Most of our awkward chat was about how I was possibly going to fill up the days of my endlessly long stay. The question seemed to worry her, too. She told me I would have chores, like walking the dogs and helping Miguel feed the birds. A friend of hers named Joan ran a bookstore, where she'd be happy to buy me books. The local high school had a swimming pool. If I liked drawing, she would get me art supplies. (I said no, politely; the world is a better place when I'm not somewhere in it doing art.)

It wasn't wilderness camp—there was no mention of kayaking or making lanyards—but that was the program. Take it or leave it.

I was bold enough to ask one question. "Uh . . ." The GM glared. How the (expletive deleted) was I going to make it through a month and a half without *uh*? "Doesn't Miguel have a daughter around my age?" I tried not to sound as desperate as I felt.

"You mean Rosie." Grandmother seemed surprised. "I suppose

she is close to you in age, yes. I believe she's eleven. How old are you, Ella?"

"Eleven."

"Ah." She looked like someone who has just been told a poodle is the same species as a terrier: she had to think about it for a minute. "What an amusing coincidence." Her face was anything but amused, though. Alarmed or uneasy, maybe—not amused. "But her parents are living separately at the moment, so she is here only some of the time. And besides, given the history . . ." She shook her head slightly.

"What history?" I asked.

The GM stood up abruptly, scraping the floor with her chair. "Perhaps another time, Ella." I didn't think that was, strictly speaking, the politest way of ending a conversation. Wasn't she breaking one of her own rules? "For now, I must do some reading. And I'm sure you're tired after your long day."

I wasn't tired at all, I was wide awake, especially after all that chocolate and the new spark of curiosity she had just lit in my mind. *What about Rosie?* I wanted to ask. *She's my only hope here!* But something in my grandmother's face made me feel I'd better leave that subject alone. For the moment.

Getting back to my room was going to be nerve-racking. Night was starting to fall, and away from the fire the air was spooky and cold. I got Lou from the courtyard—he was all licky and glad to see me, the feeling was mutual—and with him by my side, and a flashlight in my hand, I was able to be brave. Having a stomach full of cake helped, too.

Grandmother and I stood in the corridor hallway to say good night.

"Ella," she blurted. She grabbed tightly onto one of my wrists. I felt the cool metal of her rings against my skin. "I am sorry about your mother's illness. It is very distressing. I trust this treatment will help her get better. Please—" She hesitated. "Please send her my good wishes when you write to her. Now, good night."

And then she and Hildy hurried away before I could say anything but "OK—good night" to her red retreating back.

This caught me off guard. It was almost disappointing that the GM had mentioned my mother at last. I couldn't write her off anymore. Not as swiftly.

This situation was confusing, and the only person I felt like talking to about it was my mom. She would get how weird this whole setup was, having dinner with my grandmother, *this* grandmother, for the first time in my life. Even though Mom and Dad had divorced a thousand years ago, back in the time of the dinosaurs, my mother obviously knew what Violet Von Stern was like. I remembered the look on her face when I told her that's where I was going. Now I understood it.

Back in my room I tried to call her at the Seattle hospital. One ring, two, three.

I got her voice mail.

Mom still sounded strong in the recording. It was from before she got sick. As I listened to her warm, familiar voice, I started twisting the new bracelet around my wrist.

She had given it to me the last day I saw her. Mom told me

she had a graduation present for me, then reached over to her bedside table. The table was completely covered with cards from the hundred people who wanted her to get better (friends, neighbors, people at the optometry store where she worked), but somewhere in there she found a small box. She passed it to me with a shaking hand. I knew she wasn't able to leave her room at that point; seeing my surprise she said sheepishly, "Nurse Rose got this for me downstairs. But it was my idea. Go ahead! Open it."

So I did. Inside was a (fake) gold bracelet with charms around it: a heart, a star, a bunny. It wasn't my style, and was probably meant for a younger kid, but it didn't matter.

"They don't have a great selection in the gift shop here," she apologized.

"No, it's great!" I put it on. What did I care if it had a bunny on it and I was almost twelve? It was from her. "I'll wear it all the time. Thanks, Mom."

Sitting in my grandmother's weird, musty back bedroom, I touched the heart, star and bunny. I decided not to leave Mom a message. I wasn't sure what to say, and besides, I worried that if I tried to, I might start crying, which wouldn't help anyone.

The only other person I could call was Auntie Irene, who answered, thank goodness. She said things were fine but that my mom wouldn't be able to talk on the phone much for the next while, so writing letters would be best. But not to worry, it was all going according to plan and she had the best doctors and it would all be fine. And not to worry. Auntie Irene probably told me about ten times not to worry.

Which of course made me worry.

"And how is your grandmother, Ella?" she asked. "Are you getting along?"

"She's all right." I didn't see the point of telling Irene the truth—I didn't want *her* to worry, either. Why go into all the details: no TV, no Internet—in fact, no technology at all from the past ten or twenty years? (What was I going to do the whole time here? Take up knitting? Practice the piano? Grandmother didn't even *have* a piano! She had everything *but* a piano.) So I just said it was fine, but that I was pretty tired and ought to go brush my teeth and get my pajamas on. I think the normal sound of that reassured her.

When we hung up, I realized that the only thing I could do was start writing a letter to my mom, like Irene said, so I did that, telling her all about the Good Grammar Correctional Facility and all the rules I was picking up. Writing her made me feel a little bit better.

And after that I really did brush my teeth and get my pajamas on, and then without even reading I fell into a fitful sleep on the cold twin bed, a fan ticking away overhead all night long, in spite of the cold, that became a helicopter in my dreams, medevacing me back home, to my mom, for safety.

Sunday, June 20, Albuquerque
Tough to spell—and I used to
think Mississippi was hard!

Dear Mom,

Well, I'm here. You can say that much. How about you? Are you there?

I wonder if the nurses are as nice in Seattle as they are in California and if you miss Dr. Lanner. I do. It was nice of him to say I could call him if I wanted to, but I'm not sure what I would say.

OK, letter writing! Here goes. I will try not 2 use 2 much bad txt spelling. First, here are a few things I have learned since I got here. I think my stay with Grandmother will turn out to be very <u>educational</u>.

1. Do not say "What?" if you don't hear someone. "What?," which I have been saying my entire life, turns out to be all wrong. You're supposed to say "Pardon?" or even "I beg your pardon?" Like people in old-fashioned books do.

2. It is never "Me and so-and-so are . . ." The truth is, I remember you telling me this, too. So—DON'T say, "Me and Lou are worried we'll be bored out of

our minds here." DO say, "<u>Lou and I</u> are worried we'll be bored out of our minds here."

3. If someone has a lot of things in their house, DO NOT call them "stuff." "Stuff" is bad. You may say "things," as in, "Wow, what a lot of things you have!" You SHOULD NOT say, "Where did you get all this stuff?" "How do you keep track of all this stuff?" or "Why in the world do you even HAVE so much stuff?"

4. "Like," used as a filler word, was invented by the devil. (Like—whatever!)

The neighborhood is deadly, too. There are no kids anywhere nearby, unless you count whoever is locked up at the Juvenile Correctional Facility a few blocks away. It is an ugly place with barbed wire around it that I guess is a jail for teenagers when they commit crimes worse than sarcasm. The only hope is this girl Rosie, the daughter of the nice guy Miguel who works for Grandmother, but I haven't met her yet.

There's no barbed wire around here, but it does feel kind of like a prison. I call it the Good Grammar Correctional Facility. I won't get released until Grandmother has fixed up my grammar. I'm thinking of drawing a map of the whole place while I'm here, which will help me get around, and might help me plan an escape route. (JK!)

Grandmother also explained that her house is very unusual in being more than a hundred years old and made of adobe, which is basically mud. I remember when we made adobe bricks in second grade with Mr. Cooper, and Josh Green cried because he hated getting so dirty.

Anyway, you know all this already—you and Dad were here together once. I saw your names written on the wall in the room where I'm sleeping. You never told me about it!

> I love you. And I miss you like (expletive deleted).
>
> Ella

FOUR

THE
Librerery

"AHEM!"

I was on the field, and Coach was telling me I had to work harder on my soccer drill. My feet were slow and dragging, and I couldn't seem to connect well with the ball.

"Ahem!" Suddenly it wasn't Coach anymore, it was my dad, telling me I had to hurry up and get packed, because we were going out on the river. I was wishing I didn't have to go with him.

"AHEM!!!"

My eyes half opened and my brain shook itself, like a dog after a rainstorm. I finally realized I must be dreaming, and that it was time to wake up.

It must be, because some tall, awful person was standing by the foot of my bed, *ahemming* like crazy, which made Lou dip his head, his tail wagging in apology, like he or I had done something wrong.

"What—what is it?" I said blearily.

"It is time, Ella," my grandmother said, "to get up."

Suddenly I sat upright. A freeze fell over me. I could hardly breathe. Did my grandmother have bad news, is that why I had to get up? Bad news—from Seattle?

"What happened?" I asked in a panic. "Did something happen?"

"Happen?" My grandmother moved to the curtain, pulled it open and waved a hand toward the courtyard, the sky, the scattered birds. "Certainly, something has happened. It is called *morning*." Her blue eyes returned to me. "Really, Ella, you mustn't miss the best part of the day. Come have your breakfast."

I lay back down on the bed, my heart pounding. I didn't want to risk facing Mrs. Von Stern in case laser beams were coming from my eyes and I killed her with one look.

"OK." I used as calm a voice as I could manage. I practiced my breathing exercises. Coach always told us that breathing was important. "I'm coming."

It wasn't especially clear why it was so important for me to get up. It wasn't as though there was anyone with a pressing need to see me, except maybe the peacocks. Still, that was one thing I had to get used to: sleeping past seven thirty was considered an offense at the GGCF.

There was plenty else, too.

I had to get used to the food: Bran Something cereal for breakfast, which tasted like wood chips, and for dinner mushy broccoli and strange bulging sausages, along with all kinds of slaw: coleslaw, apple slaw, mystery slaw. Grandmother had a machine that shredded things into the right state for slawdom, and I wasn't always sure what had gone into its well. I glanced at the thing nervously when I had annoyed her by something I'd done, which seemed to happen about every half hour, and I wondered if one day I'd end up in the slawer myself.

I had to get used to the junk and the clutter, the way the house smelled of meat and of mildew, and to the animals, dead or alive: Hildy's high-pitched yap and watery black eyes, and poor bodiless Tigger, who I finally decided meant Lou and me no harm.

I had to get used to the peacocks: their constant cries, and the way they sometimes galloped across the roof, sounding like bandits. As Miguel had said, they didn't hurt anyone, but they did stare at you disapprovingly with their bright eyes, unless you were feeding them. That was my job now, scooping up grain from one of the feed bins or scattering compost scraps we collected in a green pail in the kitchen—slimy melon rinds, old eggshells and other delicacies.

Miguel was one of the only people who made me feel actually welcome at the GGCF. The other one was George, the UPS guy, who came almost every day to deliver more *things,* usually books (like she needed more!) but also shoes, nuts, dog food, stationery. Anything that could be shipped was shipped. (Though the boxes came by truck: why do they call it "shipping" if it comes by truck? More mysteries from the Vocabulary Department.) My grandmother was probably the only reason George ever drove into this ghost town of a neighborhood, unless the juvenile center got deliveries of handcuffs or hacksaws or whatever.

"So! You're the granddaughter!" George said the first time he saw me. He was a plump white man with matching brown hair and uniform and the tidy look of a guy from a Lego kit. "Chip off the old block, eh?" He lugged a heavy box over near the door as peacocks lurched away, glaring, like it was very inconvenient for them to have to move.

"I guess." I really hoped not, though. I didn't want to be carved from that block.

George was nice to me. He and I traded baseball news. He was a Rockies fan, but I liked him anyway. As my mom used to tell me, people can't always help what they are, and you have to accept their differences.

Someone ought to have told my grandmother that. I could tell the first time we went to her friend Joan's bookstore that she didn't feel that closely related to me, either.

Joan was a tall, big-boned redhead with a Southern drawl and a laugh like a car alarm. After we were introduced, she sat Grandmother down on a stool and then went ricocheting around like a superball, picking books off the shelves and bringing them over as if we were at a shoe store and these were sandals or boots to try on.

"I think you'll like her," Joan said, pointing at one author's toothy photo. "She's feisty. She's got spunk. Like you, Violet."

This wasn't what I was used to in a bookstore. The place my mom and I usually went was one of those vast mall-type places that sells music and movies and candy and, by the way, books, with a line of cash registers up front like at a supermarket.

"Ah!" My grandmother brightened at the sight of one book Joan had shown her. "A new history of the Waughs! What fun."

"Which wars?" I tried to sound interested.

"Oh, Ella." She rolled her eyes in exasperation. "Don't be such a philistine. The *Waughs* . . . Evelyn, Alec, Auberon . . . You sound just like your father."

I had no idea who Phyllis Stine was or how Dad managed to be like her, too, but clearly it meant something like "idiot." My eyes stung with the insult. The GM was oblivious, but Joan saw. She led me over by the shoulders to a different part of the store.

"Now, don't let your grandmother get to you," she said quietly. "Just come right back at Violet if she says something like that. Show her you've got spunk, too." Then Joan helped me toward the time-tested solution to bad feelings: reading. "Look here, hon—we've got some great new titles for juveniles . . ."

Juvenile made me think of the kids' jail again, but Joan did pick out some good books—not just the nutritious ones we'd had to read at school and then write reports about in the form of a board game or cookbook recipe. (Some teacher's idea of how to make homework more interesting.) And it was good that she did, because reading turned out to be one of the biggest entertainment features of the Good Grammar Correctional Facility. Other than books, and birds, fun activities were pretty thin on the ground.

One afternoon, about four or five days after I arrived, Miguel was out teaching me how to make a silly clucking sound the peacocks seemed to love that he called his "pea-call." It involved cupping your hands and blowing on them, like you do when you're trying to get warm, but I hadn't gotten the hang of it yet.

"You see that old hen there?" Miguel jutted his chin toward one of the brown lady birds and blew a soft little call with his hands. "That one's Carmen. She's my favorite." I nodded, though how he could tell them apart was a mystery. Carmen started to wander over to a broad, hollowed-out area behind the cluster of cottonwood trees that looked like a place an asteroid had once landed. Miguel told me that many years before, this scooped-out area had been a pond, with ducks and fish and an elegant pair of swans that swam around it. It was hard to imagine that dustbowl filled with water now.

"And you know those empty fields, out behind where the Library is . . . ," Miguel went on. "That's where the Mackenzies used to keep their horses."

"*Horses*?" I said. "Who rode them?"

"Who?" Miguel grinned. "Your grandparents, of course. And Walt."

"Seriously?"

"Oh, sure. A long time ago, when your grandfather was still alive." Miguel got a storybook look in his coffee-bean eyes. "This place was real different then, Ella. I wish you could have seen it. There were living things everywhere—it was a magical place."

I tried to picture living things around, other than peacocks and guys with delivery trucks. It was tough. It was like Miguel had this old silent movie and was putting music and color back into it. "How do you know?" I asked him. "Did you come here back then?"

"Come here?" He smiled. "My dad worked here. For your grandparents. Looking after their horses and the rest of the livestock. Oscar Aguilar." So Rosie's grandfather had worked for mine? This was news to me. "That's how come I knew your dad."

"You knew my dad as a kid?"

"Of course!" He smiled. "Walt was a little older than me, I was the kid brother in our family, you know, but—sure I knew your dad. He taught me how to bait a hook. He's the first guy I ever fished with."

Here was something Miguel and I had in common: "Walt" was the first guy I ever fished with, too.

"That was before the accident, of course. After that, everything changed. They got rid of all the animals, and—our family moved away." A cloud darkened Miguel's usually clear-skied face. "I didn't see much of your dad after that, or Mrs. Von Stern either. For a long time. It was a surprise when she got in touch after all these years and asked me to work for her." He sighed. "Rosie's mom wasn't too happy when I said yes."

I wondered if it was something they had argued about. "Why not?"

"Oh—she thinks there are bad bad spirits around the place. Because of the unhappy history."

Great. Now I was going to find it even easier to sleep at night.

I still didn't even know what had happened to my grandfather, exactly. No one ever seemed to think they needed to tell me that, or other important things. I figured Miguel might actually spill the beans at last, but before I could find out, my cell phone suddenly came alive in my back jeans pocket. "Nowhere Man," that old Beatles song.

"It's my dad," I told Miguel, like I'd forgotten I even had a dad.

"He knew we were talking about him," he said, smiling. Then he waved me to answer it and wandered off to get some real work done.

"Belle, old girl!"

Yeah, that was my dad all right. He sounded mighty cheerful for a guy who had abandoned his daughter in her hour of need. "Sorry I didn't call earlier. We were on a three-day float and there wasn't great cell coverage—"

"Uh-huh." There was always some version of this story. The exact details didn't much matter.

"—a group of businessmen from Southern California. They couldn't tie a fly to save their lives. We'd have starved if it hadn't been for the powdered eggs."

There were things I wanted to ask my dad once he quit the fisher-talk, but before I had the chance, he dropped the hearty act for a second. "So, Ella, how are you holding up? Are you and the Old Dragon getting along OK?"

"Yeah." Though *OK* seemed an exaggeration. "I mean—it depends."

"But she hasn't thrown you in the slawer yet?" I couldn't believe he had thought of that, too.

"Not yet." Then again, I'd been there less than a week. There was plenty of time.

"Well, that's a good sign." He chuckled. He always found his own jokes pretty funny.

"Dad—" I blurted. I couldn't hold back anymore. "There's nothing to *do* around here. The only game she has is Boggle. I mean, there's no Internet, there's no TV—"

"Internet?" He chuckled again. "No. Violet Von Stern is *not* wired. (Expletive deleted), Ella, you're lucky you've got a signal on your cell phone." Him and his expletives. I wondered what the GM had to say about *those*. "Listen, Belle, I understand what you're saying. Absolute. That house—I mean, I haven't been there for a long while, but it's not set up for kids. I know that much. It's an unweeded garden and all that." He paused. "Has she shown you the *Librerery* yet?" He pronounced the word with a silly snobbish accent that did sound a bit like Grandmother.

"Nope."

"Well, I'll tell you. It's kind of amazing. My mother has a thing about books."

"I noticed."

"Yeah, well, the *Librerery* has some pretty remarkable specimens, and though that may not sound very exciting—"

"It doesn't."

"OK, but I'm just saying there are some things in there worth paying attention to. You won't see them anywhere else, that's for sure. Tell her to show you Kepler's *Dream*—she has the Morris edition, Belle, and there are only a dozen copies in the whole *world*." That didn't make any sense. What sort of book only has twelve copies? "That book—well, I've had mixed feelings about it over the years, to put it mildly, but you should still see it."

"Sounds great. I can hardly wait." I hoped the sarcasm made it through the phone line. "So . . . when are you coming to visit, Dad? You said you would."

"Yeah—right. Uh—there's a chance I might be able to stop through Albujerk on a layover, on my way to Colorado. It's complicated. You know, Ella, as I think I explained to you, Mother and I don't get along too well. That is—"

I let a thick silence fill up the phone.

"Well, anyway. I'll—I'll try to figure that out, Belle. OK?"

OK, Dad, but you better mean it this time. You can't flake out on me this summer, you know? Not this *summer.* I wondered if there was anyone around who could explain that to him. Where was the (expletive deleted) dad manual when you really needed it?

That night, maybe even the GM was tired of mushy broccoli, so after a game of Boggle—it really was what passed for entertainment at the GGCF—she took me out to dinner at a French place called Chez Albertine. There was something about going to a French restaurant when I knew there had to be great Mexican food all around that felt kind of like going to Paris and ordering tacos, but whatever. At least we were *out*.

My grandmother ordered snails from the menu, "One of my favorite dishes!" I had to just pretend not to see them or I would get seriously grossed out. So over my steak and fries, for a distraction, I asked about her *Librerery*. I copied Dad's goofy pronunciation, but she didn't seem to notice.

"The Library?" Her face came into focus. "Would that interest you, Ella?"

"Sure." I mean, not as much as going *online,* or watching a *movie,* or talking to one of my actual *friends,* but . . . compared with feeding peacocks all day, yeah. *Yesssss.*

"I have to open the place up soon in any case, as two boys are coming to help me begin cataloging the collection. High schoolers." She didn't sound thrilled about this. "They come—ahem!—recommended, but I find it impossible to tell them apart or remember their names, so I think of them as Tweedledum and Tweedledee."

She said this as though it were a perfectly sensible thing to say, so I nodded, to be a good sport. "And Dad said there's some amazing book you have by, uh—Kepler?"

"Kepler's *Dream*?" My grandmother's voice was sharp as a knife edge. "Your father told you about that?"

"Well, he mentioned it . . ." I got all mumbly again. "I don't know . . ."

She looked out the window. "I thought your father found the purchase of that book extravagant," she said stiffly, but she wasn't talking to me so much as addressing the Sandias in the distance. Then she turned back. "The Morris Kepler, Ella, is an extremely rare book, the most valuable in my collection. It is a remarkable artifact. Have you ever heard of the Kelmscott Chaucer?"

"No." It sounded like the name of a racehorse. Or maybe a

famous murderer. *Did you hear that creepy story about the dude in Kelmscott? He chauced ten people before they caught him.*

"Ah. Well, it is a masterpiece of book art, and the Morris Kepler is a similarly rare volume. Your grandfather always dreamed of owning a copy one day, and some years ago—when you were a very little girl—I had the chance to realize his dream."

I knew almost nothing about my grandfather, except that he had died when my dad was a kid. I always found it weird to think of him being dead so long before I was even born. It was like thinking about infinity, or black holes—it made my brain curdle.

"Was he a collector too?"

"Edward? Edward was an astronomer." The GM's face shone with an unfamiliar light. "He loved looking at the stars. It would be fair to say he liked stars better than he liked people."

Like you and books, I thought, but kept quiet.

"He knew all their names, as if they were his friends, and he knew when they were planning to be where, in the sky. He had all their paths in his head, memorized."

"Like a travel agent," I said.

My grandmother laughed. At something *I* said! I almost choked on my steak.

"I like that, Ella. Quite right." She looked at me, seeing something she hadn't before. "Your grandfather was a travel agent to the stars. Plotting their itineraries. That's very clever."

I felt a flutter of pride.

"Edward loved Kepler," she continued in a low, almost dreamy voice. "Kepler was one of the great early astronomers and mathematicians, Ella—like Galileo. He worked out many important things, such as the paths of planetary orbits, but what Edward revered about Kepler was his wild imagination. Kepler believed the Earth had a soul, and that God shaped the planets in accordance with mathematical laws." I didn't really understand what she was talking about, but I nodded anyway. I am pretty good at math—much better at math than at making a board game or recipe about some Roald Dahl book I've read— but I had never considered God in the equation. And I had barely heard of Kepler. (Scientist? Inventor? Bookstore owner?)

"Edward used to love to tell me about the strangest and least known of Kepler's works—his *Somnium,* or *Dream.* It is Kepler's fanciful account of what the Earth might look like if we traveled to the moon. Kepler imagined moon travel more than three hundred years before it happened! Edward used to say the *Somnium* was man's first work of science fiction. Kepler brought out several crucial works in his lifetime, but the *Somnium* was only published in 1634. Posthumously."

I looked blank.

"Which means, after he died."

"Oh."

"So when, thanks to an antiquarian book dealer Edward and I had known named Christopher Abercrombie—whom you will meet next week, Ella, as he is coming to visit—the opportunity came up to buy this book, years after Edward had passed away, I leapt at the chance. Building the Library, and our collection, was my way of honoring Edward's memory. That volume is the centerpiece of a collection that Edward and I started together, while he was still alive." She looked down at her snail shells for a minute. I did not want to think about what had been inside them. "To your father, I believe, the entire project was frivolous. We have very different opinions on the subject." She looked back up at me. "In any case, Ella. Would you like to see it?"

It wasn't so much a question as a command.

"Sure!" I said, trying to muster something like enthusiasm.

So the next morning, when I came into the kitchen for my usual breakfast of playground bark in a bowl (when George finally delivered Irene's care package a week later, I could sneak handfuls of Froot Loops in my room, which is how I actually survived), there was Grandmother waiting for me at the table, her eyes as beady as Hildy's.

"Ah, Ella! Shall we set off, when you're finished?"

I half expected to see a thermos and brown bag lunch beside her. She had that jazzy, expectant look teachers get when you're going on a field trip—even if it's to somewhere tedious like the botanical gardens or the local gas and electrical plant.

I'd passed the Librerery a bunch of times when I was walking Lou. As field trips go, this one didn't involve a lot of travel: the building was only about twenty feet from the house. You just had to go through the front door, elbow a few birds out of the way, then go around the side by some deserted wooden pens half covered in brambles. "That's where I used to keep my pet skunks," the GM said casually as we went by. "Dear old Arpege and Chanel Number 5. Remind me to tell you the story one day."

Skunks? But there was no time to ask any more about that, as we trotted down a few steps and there we were.

My grandmother's key to her main house was a huge old-fashioned one, like the kind that unlocks the dungeon door in a fairy tale. But for the *Librerery* she used an ordinary key. As soon as she opened the door, there was a shrill beep, and she typed in a code for the alarm. That was something she didn't bother with at home either, even with all her *things*. It was my first hint that there must be something worth guarding in here.

It had been bright outside, and it took my eyes a minute to adjust to the dimness. The place was cool and hushed, and I suddenly felt very far away from everything. In another world.

It was one long, high-ceilinged room, shaped like a chapel. Me and my mom—*ahem!* my mom and I—weren't churchy people, but during Mom's illness, Auntie Irene had taken me along a few times to her church. It was peaceful, and I liked the singing. I didn't know how to pray, really, but I could see how going to a quiet stone building would get you in the right frame of mind to do it.

The *Librerery* seemed something like that, only instead of saints and crosses all over, there were books.

Hundreds and thousands of books.

They were everywhere. On all the shelves, from floor to ceiling, stacked or spread open on high tables and side tables and low coffee tables, or packed in cardboard in a cluttered back nook. In the center of the room were a couple of armchairs, each with a lamp beside it, like if you were in the mood, you could just plonk yourself down in one of them, get comfortable and read. For the rest of your life.

"Wow," I said.

It was not the most imaginative utterance of my life, but I couldn't think of what else to say.

"Yes, Ella." She didn't correct me, for once. "This is the Library."

The GM had, as Dad had said, a thing about books.

"Your grandfather and I bought many of these together," she told me. "I couldn't have done it alone. Edward loved books, too. It was how we met, actually, at an antiquarian bookstore—Christopher's. We were both interested in a volume of Blake."

She said that collecting started as something they did just for fun, as a hobby. Then they got interested in older, rarer books, and it became a kind of game, a sport, to find unusual editions to add to their growing library.

"Some of these books are very valuable," my grandmother explained. "Those volumes you should touch only if you have gloves on." This seemed crazy to me—wearing gloves to look at a *book*?—but it didn't seem smart to say so. "And if I ever see you do this, Ella"—she licked a finger and made a page-turning gesture, that way some people do when they read—"I won't let you in here again."

Was that a threat or a promise?

I asked the GM how you knew which were the most valuable books. She said if they were signed by an author who was dead, for instance, or inscribed ("Meaning, written in") by one famous writer to another. (She had a book by someone named Oscar Wilde that he had signed for his son, who had the wacky name "Vyvyan".) A very old book, or a book printed on special paper, or with a binding made of some fabulous ingredient, like camel hide. Or gold.

"Which brings us to Kepler's *Dream*," she said. "Would you like to see it?" It sounded like we were going to read Kepler's mind, somehow. His dream.

My grandmother solemnly led me to the end of the room, where there was a fireplace and a bucket of firewood. Something you don't often see in the school or local library—a handy place to warm up if you get chilly while you're studying.

Nearby I also noticed a long glass cabinet filled with photographs, objects, clippings. I knew I was supposed to be psyched about Kepler's *Dream*, whatever in the world it was, but the pictures caught my eye.

"Who's this?" I looked at a black-and-white snapshot of a pretty young woman seated next to a tall, silvery guy with a swanky old-time hat on.

"That"—my grandmother's face, normally sharp, blurred some as she looked at the photo—"is Edward. And myself. On our honeymoon." If I squinted, I could see how that smiling girl might one day turn into this older Violet Von Stern.

"Hey!" I saw another picture, one of the same silvery guy smiling and shaking hands with a familiar dark-haired figure. "Isn't that Michael Collins?"

"Yes, it is." My grandmother seemed impressed that I recognized him. "Edward knew the Apollo astronauts. He was an important astronomer, Ella. His work was of significant help to NASA when it was developing its space program."

Well, that was worth the price of admission right there. My own grandfather had known Michael Collins! Had shaken the man's hand! I wondered if my mom knew. A spidery chill crawled down my spine.

Suddenly I was very curious about this Edward Mackenzie. There were pictures of him with other people I didn't recognize, and medals and ribbons, and a small plaque with his name. On another shelf, a display of feathered hooks and bright-colored nylon.

"Oh, right," I said to my grandmother. "He fished, too?"

"Well, yes. He did." It didn't seem a happy subject: a frown shadowed her face as if I'd just said *What* and not *Pardon.* "But the constellations were his real passion. You know, that is why I returned to my maiden name after Edward died. Von Stern. Do you know what *Stern* means, Ella?"

I stared at her. This seemed like a setup.

"It means 'star.' In German. Edward loved the fact that my name meant 'from the stars.'" She sighed. "After he died, I couldn't bear to be a Mackenzie any more."

"And how did he die again?" I asked.

Wrong question.

"There was an accident," she said curtly, which seemed all that anyone was ever going to tell me about it. And whatever warmth had been on my grandmother's face froze right up again. "Now, do you want to see Kepler's *Dream* or not, Ella? Otherwise I should start preparing for those wretched boys. They start work soon."

"Of course!" I hopped to it.

My grandmother put on a pair of white gloves she kept in a drawer and handed me a pair, too. It made us seem like criminals trying not to leave fingerprints as we got ready for the big heist. She gave a long explanation of who Morris was, and why his edition of this Kepler book was so valuable, how many precious whatnots were part of the binding and how the prints were ever so carefully produced and many other details I would mention if I had truly been paying attention at the time, which I wasn't. My grandfather had been a fisherman, and an astronomer, and he had known Michael Collins! And he had died in some mysterious accident that no one wanted to explain to me. There were a hundred other questions I wanted to ask the GM about him, but first I had to look at her extra-special amazing book.

Grandmother cradled the copy in her hands carefully, as if it were a baby. When she opened it, I saw thick, ragged-edged pages printed in a language I didn't recognize, with vividly colored images of stars and devils and round, looming planets that looked like the earth. And the moon.

"Here, you see," she murmured. "The witch's son is given a sleeping draught and then he makes the trip to the moon, along with the demons, to see what it might be like to live there."

With the pictures and big strange writing, it reminded me of a children's book. Then I remembered that my grandmother had said it was like a work of science fiction.

Finally she showed me the title page, printed in brilliant gold leaf.

SOMNIUM SEU ASTRONOMIA LUNARI, it said at the top in large gilded letters. Below, the translation into English.

Dream or Astronomy of the Moon.

Here it was. Kepler's *Dream.*

Dear Mom,

How are you feeling? Crummy, according to Auntie Irene. She reminded me that this was always going to be the hardest part, the treatment before you get the new blood. She told me you said all the radiation is making you feel like a pizza stuck in the microwave too long. When we used to use the school microwave, Ms. Nelson always called it "nuking"—as in, "Here, Ella, why don't you nuke these caramels to melt them" the day we made caramel apples.

I don't like to think of you getting nuked.

Did our horoscopes warn us about this? I know they're about as accurate as fortune cookies, that the pattern of the stars on your birthday doesn't truly shape your future. Still, did either one of us get one that said, "Beware of this summer, for it will suck"?

Big news here, though. We are going to have a Visitor! I will no longer be the only inmate, I mean guest, staying here with Violet Von Stern. His name is Christopher Abercrombie, and he seems famous, because I see his name everywhere. Half the boxes George the nice UPS guy delivers say ABERCROMBIE BOOKS

(VANCOUVER) on them, so that's how I'll think of him, as ABERCROMBIE BOOKS.

He is English, apparently, and he and Grandmother are old pals. He'll be staying in the Haitian Room, which makes me feel sorry for him. It's dark and hot and yellow in there. It will be like sleeping inside an omelet.

It seems unlikely, but maybe he'll be better company than Miguel's daughter, Rosie. I finally met her for the first time today, but it turns out she hates me. It was pretty much hate at first sight, I'm not sure why. She got dropped off by her mom, and when Miguel introduced us, telling her I was from California and played soccer, she chewed her gum and shrugged, like, _Am I supposed to care?_ He told me Rosie rides horses at her uncle's ranch, so I said "Cool!," which was lame. When he asked me if I ride, I said "Oh sure!" which is what Ms. Nelson might call a hyperbole, or exaggeration, since the only time I ever did was when I was about four, at the pony ring at the Sonoma County Fair. Remember that? I was almost too scared to do it but you told me it would be OK, and then afterward I'm sure I went around pretending I was suddenly this great cowkid.

Miguel did say we might go riding up at this ranch sometime. So I may have an actual outing to look forward to. Maybe when we're there, I can make a break for it and take off across the mesa.

Just kidding.

I love you.

Ella

FIVE

THE
Circle C

SOME CAMPS HAVE SLOGANS. AT ABBIE'S WILDERNESS one, where you were supposed to develop survival skills, or at least summer craft skills, they told the campers, "When you can rely on yourself, others can rely on you." When she was younger, she went to more of a hippie camp up near Willits, California, where they taught you circus tricks and how to eat with your hands. Their motto was "Let the sun shine in."

So if Broken Family Camp had a slogan, I figured it was probably "Don't expect much, and you won't be disappointed."

This had other uses in life, like not getting too hyped about whether your soccer team would make the playoffs, or caring that the Giants threw away a game in the ninth inning, or being surprised that the summer's huge summer blockbuster turned out to be a dud.

In the current situation, it applied to my hopes about Rosie. I had this crazy idea that another girl around the House of Mud, even if she was only there part of the time, might help rescue me from death by boredom. That turned out to be a mistake.

The day we met, her mom was dropping her off, and her parents were obviously fighting. My grandmother had told me Miguel and his wife were "separated" not divorced, but there was still that thing where no one would look anyone else in the eye and there was a lot of angry talk in fast, low voices. After a minute a thin, pretty girl with long dark hair and a huge frown on her face got out of the car, her hands stuffed deep into her embroidered jeans. She wasn't looking at anyone—especially her dad. Or me.

There was one more quick exchange between Miguel and Rosie's mom, and then she drove off in a cloud of mad dust, leaving Rosie standing there with a backpack at her feet, her arms folded, her lower lip pushed out.

I felt bad about seeing this, because if there is one thing that's worse than your parents fighting over you, it is some random other kid witnessing your parents fighting over you. Maybe I should have just gone back into the house as if I had never been there at all, but I couldn't help wanting to lay eyes on this kid, so I stayed there with my peacock pals and waited to be introduced.

It didn't go well. Whether Rosie hated me for being the boss's granddaughter, or for my lousy haircut, or for the fact that she was going to hate anyone at all on a day her parents were at each other like cats and dogs, I wasn't sure, but there wasn't a lot of sunshine in the whole experience. I knew Miguel was trying to be nice to me by suggesting that I go riding with them up at the ranch, but from the look on his daughter's face he might as well have asked if she minded if some toddler came over and broke all her toys.

So after the Rosie disaster, I tried to get excited instead by the fact that there were going to be two high schoolers coming to work for my grandmother. Maybe, I figured, I could strike up a friendship with them?

I'm not sure what I was imagining. That we'd all kick a soccer ball together around the former pond, now dustbowl, and talk about what music we had on our iPods? That they'd lend me their laptop so I could play a few online games, and stay sane? Once I actually laid eyes on Tweedledum and Tweedledee, though, and realized that for them some eleven-year-old girl held about as much interest as a mosquito, I gave up a few more of my big dreams.

They were really called Jackson and Jason, and I wasn't sure why Grandmother confused them, because they did look different from each other. One was tall and skinny with floppy blond hair, and ate a lot of sunflower seeds, then spat the shells out everywhere, like a bird. That one was Jackson. The other one, Jason, was short, with dark hair in the shape of a helmet. He found it hard to look anywhere other than at his phone. His thumbs were on it all the time, moving at the speed of light, and then he'd sort of grin and mutter to it, too, like it was more real to him than anyone else. Which was probably true.

The first day they came they ended up disappearing with Grandmother into the Librerery, and I was back to square one for entertainment. The night before, I had finished a book about a haunted pet store, and that morning I had gotten halfway through another one about a school for werewolves, so I was pretty well done with the paranormal for a few hours at least.

I don't know where you want to draw the line between being "nosy" and being "curious." Or whether "curious" is even always a good thing. When we were doing our science fair projects, Ms. Nelson told us that curiosity was an important quality for a scientist; on the other hand, look at how much trouble that famous monkey George gets into, even if things usually work out for him in the end. As for nosiness, I never appreciated it when my mom occasionally went investigating in my room and found my secret stash of Halloween candy, or some dumb teen magazine I was embarrassed for her to see. "That's private!" I'd protest, and she'd just give me a look, like, *Not anymore, it isn't.*

Anyway, I started poking around the House of Mud. While Tweedledum and Tweedledee were off shuffling books around with the GM, I decided to set off into wild, unexplored territory. I went with Ms. Nelson's line: I was just trying to be a good researcher. I had a pad and paper with me, and was beginning to take notes for my map drawing of the House of Mud.

There was one whole side of the house past the kitchen that we never went to; it was like the dark side of the moon. After the kitchen, there was a big echoey dining room, where the GM and Edward must have fed their ghost-guests in the olden days, though a layer of dust coated all the surfaces now. I called that the Room for Imaginary Diners, since I didn't think anyone had eaten there since the era of the horses and the Aguilars. Then there was a small room with paintings and other art that seemed like a Hall of Mirrors, and finally, at the end, sharing a wall (I was pretty sure) with my musty old bathroom, was a packed place I thought of as the Chamber of *Tchotchke*s—a word I got from Abbie's mom, for trinkets and, ahem!, *stuff,* which the Lunzes also had a lot of. It was in the Chamber of Tchotchkes where I hoped to make some great discovery. A cure for cancer, maybe, or a magic wardrobe; or at the very least, more information about Edward.

So far the only thing of interest I'd turned up, though, besides an old gray rubber ball, was from a big drawer of photographs. I found one of the same silvery Edward, standing with his arm around a kid who looked a lot like the Haitian Room's penciled boy. The penciled boy, if my grandmother was to be believed, was my father, Walter. Who hadn't, I noticed, featured a whole lot in my grandmother's conversation.

I took the picture back to my room, and like a dog burying a bone I hid it under my pillow. I admit I felt like a thief, but I wasn't up to asking the GM for permission. And I wanted one small piece of proof that my dad had once had a dad of his own.

The day after I wrote my mom, a car pulled into the driveway. I was outside playing fetch with Lou with that ball from the Chamber of Tchotchkes. For all I knew the thing was an antique from England or Timbuktu—it sure didn't have a lot of bounce left—but it was good enough for fetch.

This was a regular white car, not a pickup or a delivery truck. The peacocks immediately swarmed all over it. The driver cut the engine but didn't get out right away. He was probably trying to figure out how to handle the birds.

"Don't worry," I called. "They won't peck your eyes out or anything."

The car door opened. Since the GM had called Abercrombie's store "antiquarian" I had been imagining the guy himself as ancient, hobbling around with a cane, but out stepped a short, round man with a white suit, a straw hat and a beige goatee. With his black briefcase and cagey expression, he looked something like a stage magician, getting ready to put on his show. All he needed was a white rabbit.

"You must be Ella!" The man waved—like someone in a play, pretending to be friendly. "How d'you do?"

He put out his hand and I shook it, though mine was kind of disgusting with dog spit. I saw him reach for a handkerchief and wipe his off afterward.

"Christopher!" sang a voice from the screen door. And there was the GM, decked out in a royal-blue dress, her hair done, her cherry lips smiling. Jewels at her ears and neck. She sparkled.

"Violet!" He bustled over. "How marvelous to see you. You look ravishing as ever." He stood up on tiptoes to kiss my grandmother's cheek. She was about half a foot taller than him. "And how is sweet little Brunhilda?" He stroked the dog's toy head.

"As delighted to see you as I am." Grandmother kept smiling. Her teeth looked a little like fangs. "Welcome to our humble abode. Come in."

"The hacienda! At last. I've always wanted to see the Von

Stern collection in situ." He sneezed, inspiring a "Gesundheit!" from the GM and another outing for his handkerchief. Then he rolled himself and his bags in through the screen door.

They seemed to have forgotten about Lou and me. I shrugged. "Well," I said to Lou, picking up fetch where we had left off, "I guess Abercrombie Books isn't going to be our new best friend, either."

"Ahem!" My grandmother lingered in the doorway, and by now I could figure out just by her head tilt, without her telling me, that she wanted me inside. I wasn't going to get off easy, I guess. "Come in, Ella—come meet Our Guest." *Ours*—as if I had anything to do with inviting him.

We all sat awkwardly in the kitchen, sipping iced tea, but Abercrombie Books and I used up our small talk fast. He asked me what grade I was in, so I said I was going into sixth ("Sixth grade! How marvelous!"), and he asked me whether I had any "hobbies" so I told him soccer ("Ah, yes. 'Footie'!"). I asked him how he liked living in Canada and he said, "I like it a great deal." Finally he leaned forward and with that same fake friendliness said, "And, Ella, I understand from your grandmother that you're quite a reader. I think I know who you get *that* from."

The man annoyed me. Whatever play he was in, I didn't want a part in it. "My mom loves to read too," I told him. I still found the idea of me inheriting anything from the GM highly unlikely. I had only recently met the woman. I knew genetics didn't depend on that, but still. "We usually walk to the library once a week or so. It's only a couple of blocks from our house in Santa Rosa."

"Well, here it's even closer, isn't it?"

"Christopher is *dying* to see the Library," Grandmother put in. "We'll take him on the grand tour tomorrow, Ella, shall we?"

I agreed. "We can show him the Kepler book."

"Kepler?" Abercrombie's face quivered, exactly the way Lou's does when he's seen a squirrel.

"Sure, you know—the *Dream of the Moon*." I liked sounding like I knew what I was talking about. "The one made by Morris," I added airily.

"Good Lord, Violet," he said in a low voice, as if somehow I might not hear him. "You don't let the child handle the volume, do you?"

I wanted to *Ahem!* him for calling me a child, but the GM just said, "Certainly I do. I was showing her the Library."

"But the Morris Kepler!" He sounded as though he was talking about the Crown Jewels. "You should have it in a locked case. Even Jason and his friend, while they work on the cataloging project, might be tempted—"

"Tempted?" Grandmother snorted. "No, I don't think so. I'm sorry to tell you, Christopher, but those two boys are roughly as interested in my books as Hildy is in my stamp collection." She gave him one of her stern looks. "And in any case, I don't believe in shutting away such a treasure where it can't be enjoyed."

"There are only twelve of them in the world, you know," I

piped up, but instead of Abercrombie being impressed by my knowledge, he just smirked.

"Yes, Ella. I know."

"It was Christopher," my grandmother told me, "who sold the book to me, Ella. Years ago. When you were just a little girl."

"Not that Walter was too happy about it." Mr. Books had this slippery smile on his face that I found obnoxious. "I gave you a good deal on it, as I recall. Good Lord, what must it be worth now—ten or twenty thousand—?"

"*Ahem!*" My grandmother cut him off. "It is impolite to discuss numbers, don't you think?"

Abercrombie looked away, as if he had a different thought running through his mind, but before he could say anything else, in came Miguel carrying logs for the fire, Hildy and Lou at his feet. The two dogs still weren't sure about each other—Lou thought Hildy was a wimp, and Hildy considered Lou a mutt, which he was—but they ran around the woodpile and had a good time in spite of themselves.

The two men traded brief hellos, and then Abercrombie excused himself to go to "the Gents."

"By the way, Mrs. V," Miguel said as he built the fire, "I talked to my brother today."

"Your brother?" She frowned.

"Carlos, I mean." He coughed. "*Carlos.* Anyways, he's happy for me to take Ella over to the ranch tomorrow, for a ride."

"Ah." She turned to me. "And you'd like to do that, Ella?"

"OK. Sure." I tried not to actually drool over the possibility. *Escape!*

"I imagine it won't break your heart to miss showing Christopher the Library . . . ," she said, but by now my ear was tuned in to her sarcasm, and I knew I was allowed to agree. "Fine. She'll be ready in the morning, Miguel. You'll want to go before it gets too hot, I imagine."

"Thanks, Mrs. V." He raised his hat at me. "I'll see you in the a.m., Ella. You and me and Rosie will have a great time."

Luckily he couldn't see the GM's wince at his grammar.

I got up practically at dawn the next morning, I was so eager. I put on my jeans and the new boots Abbie's mom had bought for me, and though I didn't have a cowboy hat, I hoped a Giants cap would do. I went outside after breakfast to find Miguel.

The person I found was Rosie.

She was wandering around out by the empty pond, kicking stones, popping bright pink bubble-gum bubbles. When I said "Hi," she looked startled. "Hi," she replied, with about as much enthusiasm as if I were a peacock.

She seemed different from the one other time we'd met, though. Tougher. That other afternoon, when she was being dropped off by her mom, Miguel's daughter had been in a dress, her hair in a long braid down her back. She wore pretty sandals, and a small gold stud in each ear. She was a girly kind of girl, in other words, the kind I was not, with my still-growing-out hair and my jeans-and-T-shirt combo that I had by then been granted permission to wear. One of my theories about why Rosie hated me was that she didn't like my style. Too sporty. The other one was probably truer—Rosie was just in a bad mood about her parents' separation and not about to think of the boss's granddaughter as anything but a spoiled brat.

That morning she was dressed in jeans with colorful embroidered flowers, and dusty red cowboy boots that you could tell had been around real horses. With my squeaky new boots and baseball cap I realized I didn't look like much of a rider.

"Ready, girls?" Miguel acted like Rosie and I had been palling around together, rather than standing quiet as a couple of sparrows. "Let's get in the truck. *¡Vaminos!*"

We all squeezed into the cab. Lou was inside the house barking, upset that he couldn't come too, and Abercrombie Books was in his Haitian Room, but Grandmother stood at the screen door waving, looking for a minute like a regular grandmother.

Even sitting next to a kid who had no time for me, I was pretty excited. I had been so cooped *up*. I felt like Lou when he finally got a walk after I'd been away at school all day long. When I saw a sign saying we were crossing the Rio Grande, I couldn't help saying something. I hadn't even seen the river once since I'd been there.

"The Rio Grande!" I looked out the window expecting some huge glittering blue that looked like, you know, the Mississippi. Or the Amazon. Instead I just saw a wide stretch of red-brown slurry. "Geez. It's not looking that *grande* right now, is it?"

"Not right now," Miguel said. "But you should see her farther up. Out of the city. Beautiful river." He paused. "Dangerous, too, you know. You don't want to underestimate that river."

"Dangerous?" I laughed, like he had made a joke. This water looked like something you could practically wade across if you had to. But Rosie gave her dad a dark daughterly stare for his comment, then went back to chewing her gum.

After we cleared the Rio and some neighborhoods on the other side, we started driving through more open country. The land was scrubby and dry, the earth a burnt orange. Eventually, after various swoops and curves, we headed uphill. When we came to two tall wooden posts under a sign that said Circle C Ranch, we turned.

"This is Carlos's place," Miguel said, and I could feel the air in the truck change. Happiness came into it: you could tell this was a place Miguel and Rosie loved.

Ranch might sound grassy and green, but the Circle C was all dust, wood and horses. And flies. There was a shaded indoor ring, there were trailers here and there, and kids and grown-ups walking about in their cowboy hats and boots, with places to go. By one low building was a big wood board with a list of painted rules, including, in capital letters, DON'T SCARE THE HORSES!

"My dad says you like to ride?" Rosie asked me. Since it was pretty much the first question she had ever directed my way, there was only one thing to do.

I had to lie.

"Oh, yeah." I gazed off into the distance, as if I were imagining life back at home in Santa Rosa, and how much riding I did there.

"Do you have a horse?"

"Oh, yeah." I nodded. "Yup. He's called—he's called Kepler."

"And what is he—a Pinto? Palomino?"

She seemed interested, so I had to keep going. "Uh—yeah. That's right. A Pinto Palomino."

She gave me a weird look. (Later, when I knew more about horses, I realized it was like I had just told Rosie that my mom drove a Hummer Mini Cooper.)

Luckily I didn't have to say any more about Kepler because Carlos showed up, a guy in a huge white cowboy hat with a thick black moustache. There were loud greetings all around— a big hug for Rosie, a slap on the back for Miguel, a surprised laugh for me.

"Look at you!" he said. "You're Walt's daughter—yes, you are." He looked over at Miguel, who was nodding his agreement. "Let's hope she rides better than Walt, though, huh, bro?" And the two of them shared some memory with their eyes that the rest of us could only guess at.

Carlos's teenaged daughter Lola had saddled up some horses for us near one of the barns. There were going to be five of us on the ride: Rosie, Lola, Miguel and Carlos—and me.

When we ambled over there, I felt my knees go a little weak. Rosie seemed so comfortable and confident, and Carlos talked to each horse like they were members of his family. I was guessing that I might be looking exactly like what I was: a dumb girl from California trying to fake her way into a trail ride with people who knew better.

"Now, I know Miguel told me you've ridden some," Carlos said to me, falling in step alongside. He smelled like cigarettes and horses—kind of a nice combo, believe it or not. And he had a warm voice like Miguel's. "But I've put you on a real gentle mare anyways, so you can enjoy yourself. She's called Paloma, and she is, too, she's just like a dove. She's a sweetheart; you won't have any trouble with her."

"Thanks." I imagined some small, cute picture-book pony. But when I saw her, all saddled and ready, Paloma was a giant gray creature, more like a camel or a dinosaur than a horse. My palms started sweating.

Lola helped me up from the stool and got all my straps adjusted. She handed me a helmet, too, which was embarrassing since everyone else was in a cowboy hat, but whatever. I wasn't going to fight it. I still felt pretty cool sitting up there. I was on top of the world! I decided to stop worrying. Paloma felt good under me. Huge, yes, but as Carlos had said, gentle. I patted her neck, like I saw Miguel doing to his horse, and put one hand on the saddle horn, like a regular old cowgirl.

I was ready. I mean, I thought I was. I felt like I was in some kind of movie, where I could forget my troubles and ride across the Wild West looking for bandits, or gold, with a big blue sky above me and my posse by my side.

The movie lasted about ten minutes.

So here's a piece of advice I will give you free of charge. Don't, if you can help it, lie to horse people about how much riding experience you have. It isn't worth it.

Best case scenario: they can tell right away what a fake you are as you joggle along on the horse's back and can't keep the animal from stopping to eat dry weeds every five seconds, and no amount of clicking your teeth or kicking its fat sides seems to persuade it to keep going, like everyone else's is doing, so you have to wait a lifetime, getting left farther and farther behind, until your horse decides on its own to move.

Worst case scenario: you finally get the horse into a trot to catch up, and from there it makes up its own mind to lope, for no reason, and you tear past everyone else on the trail, and then because your balance is so bad, when the horse spooks at some random bird or thistle, you slide right off, landing flat on your back in a huge cloud of humiliating dust.

That's what happened to me.

For a minute I was too winded to cry, or breathe, or say anything at all. I couldn't move. I heard some shouts, and the sound of horse hooves, and pretty soon they were all surrounding me, staring down. I felt like a piece of roadkill. Miguel jumped off his horse and kneeled next to me, trying to find out if I'd broken anything.

"I'm OK," I managed to force out. "Sorry. I don't know—" He gave a little wave and shook his head, like I shouldn't try to finish the sentence.

The two girls, Lola and Rosie, stayed calm on their horses.

"You all right?" Lola asked. She had sunglasses on, so I couldn't tell her expression.

"Yeah." Even if I couldn't exactly breathe just yet.

"I fell like that a couple of times," Rosie said. "When I was first starting to ride."

She didn't have to spell it out for me: she had figured out I was a beginner.

Carlos rode over too. He had managed to lasso Paloma, who was standing there, snorting through her hot nose—like *she* was the one who had a right to be annoyed. Carlos and Miguel exchanged some sentences in Spanish over my head, coming up with a plan. Then Miguel told me that Carlos was going to take me back to the ranch while the others continued their ride.

I was so ashamed now that I just wanted to curl up in the corner of someone's stable and hide. I couldn't look Miguel in the face. It was one thing to have lied to Rosie, who didn't think much of me anyway, but I felt bad about telling Miguel I had ridden a lot when I obviously hadn't. He helped me to my feet and I kept saying I was OK, so at last he and the cousins rode off and it was just me and Carlos and Carlos's big black horse Mountain. And our old pal, Paloma.

"You want some water, Ella?" Carlos offered me a flask, and I took a big gulp. He was a big, wide guy, but he kept on talking to the two horses in a soothing murmur, telling them that we were going back to the barn soon and not to be startled and where did you think you were taking this girl anyways, Paloma, to Arizona or what?

When I handed it back to him, I saw my charm bracelet had gotten all caked in dirt. "I'm sorry," I said again to Carlos. I tried to wipe clean the heart, the star, the bunny—and before I knew it, I was crying.

And once I started, I couldn't stop.

I really *was* sorry—for being such an idiot, and about a bunch of other things, too. Carlos patted my arm and my sweaty hair (we had taken the helmet off to make sure my head hadn't split in two, which it hadn't). He gave me his red bandana to wipe my face.

"Hey, it's OK," he said in a gentle voice. "It'll be OK." He looked out over the mesa, waited for a minute, then added, "Ella, I wanted to tell you—I'm real sorry about your mom, her cancer and everything. That has got to be tough."

I nodded.

"I hope she pulls through." He brushed his hand over his thick moustache. "I'll pray for her. We all will."

I nodded again. All over the place there were people praying for my mom. I just had to hope the praying would work.

"Now," Carlos continued as my tears finally slowed down. "When you've caught your breath again, I'll help you get back on. What do you say?"

"You mean—on the *horse*?" I sniffled in disbelief.

He laughed. "Well, I don't mean on a ambulance." He touched my arm. "Listen, I'll have her on a lead rope and I'll have the reins. She won't go anywhere with you. She'll just follow me and Mountain, nice and easy, I promise. We'll get us back to the barn that way. All right? Be good for you—you don't want to get all intimidated. Not of sweet Paloma." He chucked his chin in her direction and the horse made a *harrumph* sound back to him. Kind of affectionate. "You and she ought to be friends."

So I did it. Refastened the helmet, brushed myself off, and Carlos gave me a leg up to get back on. It was a shock to be up there again. I was scared and shaky at first, but with Carlos back on Mountain and leading Paloma slowly by the reins, it was a mellow ride, just as he promised. Kind of like those pony rides at the Sonoma County Fair, in fact.

Carlos didn't say much until we were back around the barn area, when he mentioned casually, "You just need a few lessons, Ella, that's all. Then you'll be fine. I'll get Miguel to talk to your grandma about it."

"Lessons?" I squeaked. "You mean, you'd let me come back here?" I had been guessing I was going to be escorted off the property under armed guard or something. End up at the juvenile facility for lying about my horse-riding capabilities.

Carlos made a face. "Come back? What are you talking about, girl? By the end of the summer, we'll have you loping past Miguel—and meaning it. Now, help me get the tack off these horses, will you? Let's hose 'em down, even though they didn't get too hot. Mountain loves his morning shower."

So I helped Carlos clean up the horses and get them back in their stables, and at the end he gave me a few Life Saver mints, of all things, to give Paloma so we could "kiss and make up," as he put it. I held them on my hand and felt her warm feathery nose on my palm as she vacuumed up the candy. For a second I could believe what he had said, that me and this horse—*ahem!* this horse and I—might one day be friends.

"All right, Paloma," I whispered to her so no one could hear me. "I'm willing to pretend this never happened if you are."

The others came back after a while, looking tired and happy, and some more Spanish flew around between Carlos and Miguel, and I guess it was decided that Miguel would take me back to the GM's and Rosie would stay there and have lunch at the ranch. There were mouthwatering smells coming from the big house, where Lola's mom was cooking. Mexican food, of course. I knew I didn't have a chance of eating with them. I was doomed to go back to the House of Slaw.

Lola went off to do her own thing, but Rosie, before she went inside, gave me a little wave. She looked halfway friendly for a minute. Why shouldn't she? She was about to have a delicious lunch, and she knew my butt was going to be sore for days. She had seen me flattened in the dust like a lonely beetle. It must have been kind of funny.

"Bye," she called out. "See you around."

Maybe there was some possibility between us after all.

SIX

MIDNIGHT
Party

June was ending, finally. We were coming up on the Fourth of July.

In Santa Rosa we usually had music or games at the fairgrounds around Independence Day, and a few fireworks, but nothing too fancy. With luck you'd get cotton candy out of the experience, maybe some popcorn. It was always really hot, and Lou spent most of the night hiding under the bed because he hated the sounds of explosions.

This year, though, the day had a special significance: it was the date of the stem cell transplant, when my mom got her new blood. The story was, once they had radiated the heck out of her and she was totally nuked, they could give her the new, better blood that was supposed to cure her. Who knows how they think up these things, but from what Dr. Lanner had told us, the procedure could work miracles. (Which in Mom's case was what we needed.) I called her that morning. She said she had seen the stuff they were going to give her hanging in clear plastic bags and it looked like tomato juice. I think she was trying to make a little joke about it, but I couldn't get that picture out of my head, these mad doctors in Seattle injecting my poor mom with tomato juice. From that point on, the chance I'd ever drink a glass of the stuff was zero.

Usually after I talked to my mom, I had a huge urge to watch TV or some dumb YouTube video, but at my grandmother's house all I could do was play Jewel Quest on my phone, so I did that for a while, in secret. The GM wasn't supposed to know I had a Jewel Quest habit. I had no doubt that would be on her long list of unworthwhile activities.

I wasn't trying to be sneaky as I soft-footed my way to the kitchen. First of all, you never knew when my grandmother's hearing was going to be good—when, for instance, the noises I made chewing, or closing a car door (*"Must* you slam it so, Ella? Are you *eager* for the doors to fall off?"), would drive her crazy; and when she was going to be half deaf, like when I was trying to tell her something that happened to me that she suddenly couldn't hear. "Do stop mumbling, Ella, it's impossible to understand what you're saying. The *hmm-hmm* ran away with you, and you fell on your *hmm-hmm* . . . ? Tell me again."

Anyway, that morning, post–Mom talk, I thought I might as well find some banana peels or bread crusts to give to the peacocks. But I stopped when I saw that the kitchen door was shut. Behind it, I could hear my grandmother's voice: loud, bossy and not especially friendly. Whom was she talking to?

I kept quiet and stayed still.

"Well, what you don't understand is that while he's here—

Now, there is *no* need for that kind of language. The point I'm trying to make—"

It couldn't be Abercrombie Books. She never spoke to Dear Christopher in this tone.

"The timing is *inconvenient*. It would be inconsiderate. You can't just arrive somewhere without giving someone notice! Planning is not your strong suit, I know, but—"

I realized she must be on the phone. That would explain the louder voice, too.

"It is not as though you haven't already imposed a great deal on me this summer, Walter, and—"

Walter. That was my dad!

"—while I sympathize with poor Ella's circumstances, of course, it has hardly been easy—"

"Having a little listen-in, are we?" came a sly voice at my shoulder.

I nearly had a heart attack.

It was Abercrombie Books. He must have slithered in from the Haitian Room without my hearing him.

"I—I was just—" I stuttered. Oh, I hated him! And he was going to make me miss the best part now, on top of everything else.

"I wouldn't, Walter. I am warning you. It is not a good idea. Wait until—"

"Some people might call this . . . *spying*," Abercrombie whispered in the same snaky voice. He seemed incredibly pleased with himself for catching me.

"Well, don't," came the voice from the kitchen. "That is my last word on the subject. *Don't.*"

There was the sound of a receiver being slammed down.

Suddenly the door opened, and there was the GM, looking highly irritated—the more so when she discovered Abercrombie Books and me right in the corridor.

"Good heavens!" she exclaimed. "What on earth—?"

"Violet," Abercrombie said, flustered. "I was just trying to tell your granddaughter—"

"You weren't eavesdropping, were you?" The GM's voice was harsh, but directed at both of us. Her eyes were the blue of an iceberg. "It's a loathsome practice."

"I didn't hear anything." I held up my hands, as if to show that they were empty.

"Er—no, no." Abercrombie glared at me. "Neither did I."

"Good," my grandmother said curtly. "That was not a conversation for others to hear. Now, Christopher, are we to meet with Tweedle—that is—"

"Jason and Jackson, yes." At least someone around here knew what they were really called. "The boys are going to give us a progress report. And then a *prognosis*: how long they think it will take to correct and digitize the accounting of your inventory."

Grandmother nodded, but seemed hardly to hear him. "My library, Ella," she said, as if in answer to some phantom question, "holds an extraordinary and valuable collection of books, though *some* people"—here she glared, as if I were one of them; it was probably Phyllis Stine and her ilk she was referring to, I figured—"find this hard to understand. It is to catalog and order this collection, a task long overdue, that I hired . . ." She gestured impatiently toward Abercrombie.

"Jackson and Jason," he supplied.

"Precisely, Jason and Jackson. And it is also why Christopher so kindly came all this way this summer, so that he could consult with me about it—a plan that we could not easily change, incidentally, just because you were coming here, too."

This was pretty unfriendly, even for my grandmother. I blinked. She did, too, and I had the sense that she suddenly noticed that it was me, a kid, standing there, not my dad. Sometimes grown-ups' fights were like that, I'd noticed: they kept at it with each other even after the other person was gone or no longer on the line. After my dad's occasional visits in California, my mom used to carry on muttering for a day or two, to no one in particular.

"In any case." The GM tried to fix her voice—take it down the dragon scale a few notches. "Would you like to go see a movie today, Ella?"

"A what?" I figured I must have feathers in my head and misheard.

"A movie." She didn't even correct the *what*. "Joan offered to take you sometime, if you'd like, and today seems a good day for it."

A movie? A *movie*? A MOVIE??!!

"Uh, yeah. *Yes*. I would, Grandmother. That sounds fun. Thanks."

"Good. I'll call her and let her know, and she can come and collect you."

At last we agreed on something!

I had been screen starved for so long by this point that the idea of a movie made me giddy. I was so excited that I went outside to tell the birds the good news and give them the celebratory banana peels. They were happy for me, I could tell.

"Here, chick-chick-chick-chick-chickens," I called out, trying to do something like Miguel's "pea-song." I liked to call the peacocks chickens so they didn't get too snobby, thinking they were better than everyone else. "Here you go."

A little embarrassing to be caught doing that when up the driveway came two teenager-sized clouds of dust swirling around Tweedledum and Tweedledee. Jackson and Jason, as at least their own moms must call them.

"Hi," I said like a normal person, but high school boys, I don't know if you know any, aren't normal people who say something simple, like "Hi," back to you. The dark-haired one, whose thumbs were a blur of activity, didn't even look up, but the taller, blond floppy-haired one—who wore a starry T-shirt that said POLARIS: FIND YOUR TRUE NORTH—said some small syllable like "Hey" or "Eh" before spitting out a bunch of sunflower-seed shells in the direction of a few peacocks. They darted away, then circled back to peck at the remains.

"Come on, dude—we've got to get in there," Sunflower said. Texty grunted vaguely, and the two of them shuffled up toward the door.

To Texty I was still invisible, but Sunflower half nodded at me, which might have meant "Bye" in his language. I never knew when these boys were coming or going, but they paid so little attention to me, it hardly mattered. The idea that they were using computers to somehow sort through the GM's books seemed to me a bit like trying to use a scooter to scale Mount Everest, but whatever. It was a summer job. It wasn't like either of them had the personality to be a friendly barista, or a swim lesson instructor at the local pool. I wondered if they used white gloves while they worked, or if they ever illegally licked their fingers before turning a page, when no one was looking.

After that brilliant social encounter I was ready for more, so it didn't seem surprising somehow that Rosie's mother Adela should pull up soon after to drop Rosie off. I wondered if Rosie was going to gloat about my fall, or even ask how I was doing, but when she got out of the car, she slammed the door so hard, it made my efforts with Grandmother's big boat look like little love taps.

Miguel trotted over and tried to give Rosie a hug, but she pulled away and skulked off to the cabin. She didn't even glance at me. I began to wonder if I had been given a magical invisibility cloak without knowing it, which was why everyone suddenly seemed able to see right through me. Then again maybe Rosie just had more divorce mess to deal with; that produces a lot of bad tempers. Miguel went over to talk to Adela, who was still sitting there in her car. There were more rapid, low voices.

"He said he'd try to come before the Fourth," I heard Miguel say, "but you know how reliable he is." Adela replied with something that made him laugh. Miguel put a hand on the side of the car and then knocked on it lightly, like, *OK, see you later*. She drove away. Not mad this time, though, I don't think. The air was easier.

Grandmother's driveway was like a parking lot, because at the same time a VW pulled up, honking like it was coming to a party.

"Hey, you two!" Joan called cheerfully from the driver's seat. Phew: someone could see me, after all! "Shoo, you pesky pea-things. What do you say, Ella? You ready for the movies?"

"I sure am." I found it hard not to go into a Southern accent around Joan. It was sort of contagious.

"How about it, cowboy?" she hollered over to Miguel in a friendly way. "You and your girl want to join us?"

"Oh, thanks, but Rosie and me are going to have a picnic up in the Sandias." He tipped his hat to us. "You ladies have fun, though."

"You know we will." Joan waved good-bye. "All right. Buckle up, Ella. I don't need to come in and speak with your grandmother. She gave me permission to kidnap you for the day and skip all the social niceties. Much as I'd lo-o-o-ve to talk more to the divine Mr. Abercrombie." She rolled her eyes, and I giggled. The GM had brought Abercrombie to the bookstore the day before, and the meeting had not been a success.

"I love your grandmother, you know I do," Joan said as we drove away. "But she doesn't have a whole lot of sense of what it's like to be a child. I told her the other day, 'Violet, you've got to get this child to a mall!' And she said, 'Whatever for?' I had to tell her: 'Ella doesn't live on books alone, like you and me, Violet. The girl needs a movie! She needs to go shopping! Take her to a mall, for pity's sake! If you won't, I will.'"

"Thanks," I said to Joan. "You saved my life."

"Mrs. Von Stern knows an awful lot—there are some incredible things Violet knows about, from all her travels and reading and conversations—but on the subject of how an eleven-year-old spends her time, the woman is sorely underinformed."

I could only agree. Then, as I stared out at the wide streets of Albuquerque, I asked Joan if she could tell me something about my grandmother.

"Why, sure, hon. What do you want to know? I'll give it my best shot."

I thought of that harsh voice on the phone. "Why don't she and my dad get along?"

Joan whistled. "Makes sense you'd ask about that." She sighed. "First of all, sometimes it's easier to be a person's friend than it is to be their relative. I have some kin in Louisiana, and I love them and all, but let me tell *you* . . ." She shook her head. "Well, never mind about that. I don't know your daddy, Ella, so I only know one side of the story, and believe me, with families there are always at least ten sides to every story."

She went on to tell me the Von Stern side, which was that years ago, maybe almost ten years ago, my grandmother had gone out to visit dear old Mr. Abercrombie on the occasion of her finally buying a book she had hankered after for a very long time.

"Kepler's *Dream*?" I asked.

"That's the one." Joan said Mrs. Von Stern was so pleased and excited about her "biblio-find" that she stopped on her way back from Vancouver to show it off to her son. My dad had been going up to do fishing trips in Washington during the summer at that point, but was just then deciding he would stay living there full-time and leave us in California—in other words, that he and my mom were going to divorce. My mom had come up to Washington, too, to talk it over with him. It was a typical case of family members getting their wires crossed: Grandmother came for a visit just as my dad and mom were fighting about the future, and to make things even more complicated, there was a little tyke around.

That would be me.

And there was Dad thinking his mother ought to pay more attention to her little granddaughter Ella, and there was Grandmother showing off her Morris Kepler, and, as Joan put it, "I reckon your daddy just about threw that book right back in Violet's face."

That was hard to picture, it seemed a little violent for my dad, but Joan explained that she meant the phrase only "in a manner of speaking." "All I really mean is," she clarified, "they didn't see eye to eye on it."

Well, I wasn't going to let Joan quit there. I stared at her for more details until she gave in and said, "Oh, all right. Listen, I don't want to be the family gossip here, but I think the two of them each had their way of remembering Edward, and that's what they fought about. It was grief really, still, I think, and the divorce didn't help anything, either. Your daddy ended up telling Violet that she cared more about books than she did about people. She couldn't forgive him for that, and from then on she cut herself off. From all of you." She sighed. "Not that your daddy didn't have a point. You know, Ella, however important books are—and listen to me, I run a bookstore, I make my *livelihood* from books—they can never take the place of flesh and blood. That is," she corrected herself, "they *shouldn't*."

"Wait a second." My brain was trying to process everything Joan had just told me. "So you mean, I was there? My grandmother and I *did* meet once before?"

"Sure. That one time." Joan shook her head. "Should have been more, of course."

This story made sense of a few things, like Mom's comment in the hospital when I told her my vacation plan, something about what had gone on the other time. And Miguel giving me that sideways look the day he picked me up, when I said this would be the first time I'd ever met Violet Von Stern.

"I heard them fighting on the phone today," I told her. "It sounded like she was telling my dad he shouldn't come here to visit."

"*Tchhhh!*" Joan made a sound like a steam-train whistle. I wasn't sure if it was disbelief, disapproval, or both. We pulled up at the multiplex, and by that point, I was ready to throw myself into princesses or monsters or teen drama—whatever they had. "You know, hon, all I can say about that is, I bet your daddy is just as stubborn as Violet. Those things run in families."

She squeezed my hand for a second. "Enough of all that! Let's enjoy the show. Popcorn and soda are on me—your grandmother doesn't have to know a thing about it."

I had a great time with Joan. The darkness blotted out all the confusion that was going through my head, and I had never had a large root beer that tasted so good. Afterward we cruised around the mall for a while, looking not buying, just yakking about stuff. Joan made me laugh. She reminded me of an Irish setter that belonged to a friend of my mom's—big and red and funny and enthusiastic about everything. By the time we headed back to the House of Mud for dinner with Abercrombie and the GM, I felt ready to face anything—even liver. But out of nowhere there were barbecued spareribs for dinner. My favorite! I guess I had to get lucky at least once.

The grown-ups talked, grown-uppily, while I sat and listened to a replay in my mind of the GM on the phone with my dad. (Her voice had been so cold, like the air in a forgotten basement.) Eventually the table conversation turned to travel, a subject my grandmother always enjoyed. Whenever the talk ran dry between us, during our long nights of slaw together, I had learned to ask her about some of the places she had been. It always perked her right up.

"I'm beginning to plan my next trip," my grandmother announced. "And I am happy to take suggestions from the table about where I should go."

Abercrombie Books said London. For the books, of course. "You could visit Lovelace's in Cecil Court. It's a dreary little place, but he does have some surprising treasures . . . I should know. He got a few of them from me." Joan said Egypt to see the pyramids, but the GM waved a hand, saying, "Oh, the *pyramids*," in a way that made it unclear whether she had already seen them, thought they were overrated, or what.

When it was my turn, I said she should go to Peru.

"Peru!" the GM exclaimed. "What do you know, Ella, about Peru?"

I tried to remember that time my mom and I were sitting together at the desk at home, playing the Vacation Game, looking things up online. It felt like an eon ago.

"Machu Picchu is supposed to be amazing," I said hesitantly. My grandmother was staring at me, like the judge in some TV contest. "The ruins are incredible. The Incas"—I remembered it, in pieces—"made the whole place like an observatory. To watch the stars. The light fell in a special way on the buildings during the equinox, and they performed their rituals then."

A hush fell over the table. Of astonishment, I guess. I don't think anyone, except maybe Joan, believed I knew anything much.

"She sounds a little like Edward," murmured Abercrombie.

My grandmother nodded.

"My grandfather?" I asked him. I had forgotten that Abercrombie knew him, too.

"Yes, of course. An impressive man," Abercrombie Books said, though his voice was cool. "I knew Edward before I knew Violet, in fact."

"It was at Christopher's bookshop," the GM added, "that Edward and I met."

Abercrombie and I looked at each other with more curiosity than we had been able to muster before.

"Well, Ella," my grandmother said, "I have to say I think your presentation was the most successful. Peru will now be on my short list of potential destinations. I can't quite see myself hacking through the jungle, but I'll research the possibilities."

"Doesn't she win a trophy, Violet? A ribbon, at least?" asked Joan.

A trip to Hawaii? A flat-screen TV?

"She wins a slice of cake," was the GM's answer. "As do we all."

The whole dinner was about the best since I had arrived, but what with hearing about my father and grandmother arguing like cats and dogs, and the stimulation of a mall and a movie and Super Ball Joan—and knowing, in the back of my mind, that Mom was about to have pints of tomato juice poured into her veins somewhere in Seattle—it had been a long day. I was glad to take Lou on a spin around the premises, then crash early. It seemed like for the first time since I had arrived in New Mexico, I might actually get a good night's sleep.

Ha!

I might have, if it hadn't been for that little incident I mentioned earlier.

Because this was the night I heard the midnight scraping at my bathroom door, from Rosie all alone outside, sitting on a broken old cooler, waiting to tell me that Miguel had disappeared. This was the night I made up for getting caught eavesdropping by not getting caught tiptoeing at a millimeter a second all through the house in the pitch dark, and wandered out to find Rosie with only starlight to guide me. This was the night I looked up at the Big Dipper, wishing I really were like Edward Mackenzie and could read patterns and knowledge—and maybe even the future—in all those constellations.

And this was the night we heard Miguel's gun go off. The shot, the alarm wail, the dogs barking and the high, scared cry of the birds.

By the time we were crowded in the front hallway of the House of Mud and Miguel was at the front door, he had a strange, haunted expression on his face. He seemed about as spooked as the rest of us. The alarm was blaring like crazy, the police were coming and my grandmother, once she was in her gold robe, was asking Miguel to go with her out to the Library. I tended to agree with Our Guest that it might be better if they waited, but as we all knew, you couldn't say no to Violet Von Stern.

Those were long seconds, waiting in the corridor with Christopher Abercrombie, Rosie and Lou. Although Rosie and I had been hanging out together earlier, in the dim firelight of Miguel's cabin, now we had a hard time even looking at each other. I don't think she was too happy that her dad had gone back out-side. Who could blame her? And though we were all relieved when the GM and Miguel came back safely, the air got about ten degrees colder when we heard that Kepler's *Dream* was gone.

The police who showed up that night, though, were mostly interested in making sure no one had been murdered. They had heard something about gunfire and gotten all up in arms—three cars showed up, their lights spinning dramatically—and seemed sort of disappointed when my grandmother told them those had just been warning shots, fired by Miguel. One uniformed guy hung around to interview Miguel about what he had seen, or thought he had seen, while a couple of others went out to rootle around in the tangled bushes and see if there were any bad guys lurking there.

The last one, a lucky chief named Officer Barker, a guy who seemed to be wearing a hand-me-down uniform that didn't quite fit him, was the one left with my grandmother. The two of them went together, protected by the fearless Hildy, back to the Library so she could tell Officer Barker what she thought was missing.

The chief's walkie-talkie kept making loud, scratchy noises, and every now and then he would speak some mysterious code into it. It was exciting. By staying a few feet behind, I was al-lowed to come, too. That is, both adults half pretended they couldn't see me and seemed willing to ignore me if I kept quiet as a mouse. (Or, if I think about how loud the mice in our pantry used to be, even quieter.) I was still in my pajamas, but by now

I had grabbed a jacket, and I decided not to worry about impressing Offcer Barker with my wardrobe selection.

The Librerery looked almost exactly like it had the last time I'd been in there. Maybe the piles were in slightly different places, but it was the same mixture of order, clutter and paper.

There were, though, no signs of a break-in, no damaged locks or papers in disarray. Officer Barker pointed that out first thing.

"Nonetheless," Grandmother said to Officer Barker in a schoolteachery voice, "I can tell someone has been in here."

"How?" he demanded.

"Well, the door was ajar," she said sharply. Mrs. Von Stern wasn't used to people questioning her. "When Miguel and I came over to take a look, it pushed right open."

"I beg your pardon, ma'am." Barker shook his head. "But someone might have left the door open earlier in the day."

"Impossible." The GM ignored Barker's doubtful shrug. "Besides, it became clear immediately that someone had been here when I looked for the single most valuable volume in the entire library." She paused for effect. "It's gone!"

"Really?" Barker didn't seem that impressed by her announcement. He surveyed the place, taking in the hundreds and thousands of volumes. "You pretty sure about that?"

"Positive!"

"OK." Officer Barker nodded. You could tell what he was thinking: *This old lady might have accidentally left a book anywhere in this mess and who would know the difference?* But he wasn't going to stand there and argue with her. Not with fierce

Hildy glaring at him, too. "We aren't going to do anything about this tonight, Mrs. Stern—"

"*Von* Stern."

"Mrs. *Von* Stern. You'll need to go down to the station and file a report in the morning. They'll be able to get all the paperwork started for you, and we'll go from there, and get right on this."

She raised an eyebrow. I'm sure even in police language that means *Yeah, right*. "The Juvenile Correction Center is very near here, as you know, Officer," the GM said. "And while we've never had trouble from that quarter before, do you not think it worth some of your time to check in at the facility, to make sure nothing unusual has gone on there tonight?"

Now it was Barker's turn to look skeptical, though he was a little politer about how he did it, jutting out his lower jaw and making a small smacking sound with his lips. "All due respect, Mrs.—uh—*Ma'am,* books aren't usually the top items young offenders go after."

My grandmother glared at him.

"But irregardless of that . . ." he went on.

"Regardless," she corrected him sharply. "'Irregardless' is non-standard usage."

He blinked. "The point is, what might seem initially to you or I like a break-in . . ."

"You or *me.*"

"What?"

"'You or me'—'what might seem to you or *me* like a break-in . . .'"

He shook his head. Poor Barker. He might have been a policeman, and used to dealing with all kinds of thugs and robbers, but he had never had to handle the director of the Good Grammar Correctional Facility. "Yeah. Like I said," he muttered. The guy looked ready for some backup. "Anyways, the point I'm trying to make is, these things often turn out to be an inside job. And in the end there's not a whole lot the police can do about it."

"You're suggesting that someone I know took this volume that is worth . . ." At this point the GM noticed me—I was watching the Barker–Von Stern matchup from the corner—and she decided against giving a number. ". . . a *great deal* of money?"

"Yeah." He nodded. *Yeah* was also incorrect, something Barker probably didn't realize, but luckily for him she let it go. "That's what I'm suggesting. Have you hired anyone new lately? You know—any new housekeepers or anyone else at all?"

My grandmother looked at me warningly. As if I had any intention of saying anything! I just waited for her to tell Officer Barker about Tweedledum and Tweedledee. The problem was, I was pretty sure she had never gotten around to learning their actual names.

But a curious thing happened. The GM narrowed her eyes, looking around the Library as if for the first time, just as Officer Barker had.

"Yes, I see what you mean," she said vaguely. It sounded like she was considering something else. "I understand your point. I'll think that over."

Was she agreeing with Officer Barker? Or was she beginning to lose faith that he and his team were going to get the job done? Maybe she was thinking she would have to find the *Dream* thief herself. Maybe she was hoping brainy Ella Mackenzie would help her!

"Thank you, Officer Barker." He looked relieved that the GM had managed to be polite at last. "It's been a long night. I feel my granddaughter ought to get to bed. We all should, in fact."

"Yes, ma'am," he agreed. We made our way out of the Librerery. When the policeman and I were outside, she went back in to set the alarm and close up.

Officer Barker watched her, frowning. "That alarm should have been on during the night, right?" he said.

"Yes," I chipped in. I didn't really think he was talking to me, but I wanted to be helpful.

"But it wasn't the library door that triggered the security system." He took a quick look at his notes. "That wasn't the code the company received. I thought Wilson said they got a general alarm. Someone hit the panic button."

The GM, back beside him, didn't argue with the officer on this one.

"Yes, that was I," she said. "I heard the sound of the shots outside, and I became alarmed. So—I sounded the alarm." She laughed feebly at her little joke.

This was weird; my grandmother hadn't mentioned pulling the alarm herself until that moment. I was beginning to think I ought to start taking some notes, too. There were already a few things in this case that didn't add up. (Why had Miguel left his cabin in the first place? Why hadn't the library alarm gone off?)

But like I said, though I was good at math, the middle of the night was a bad time for adding anything up, and the GM was right that I needed to get to bed. Rosie and Miguel had disappeared back to his cabin. I had to go into Our Guest's room again—it was a design flaw in the House of Mud that you had to go through Haiti to get to where I slept—but I was ready to be back under my musty old blankets, with Lou at my feet.

Usually the main thing I had to worry about before going to sleep at night was whether I would have nightmares about my mom. Now there was something new troubling my brain: what in the world might have happened to my grandmother's rare copy of Kepler's *Dream.*

SEVEN

THE AGUILAR AND
Mackenzie Agency

I SLEPT LATE THE NEXT DAY. NOT THE BEST START TO MY new career as a detective, as it meant I missed seeing Abercrombie's expression first thing the morning after the theft. As far as I was concerned, *Darling Christopher,* who had talked about the Morris book as if it were the Crown Jewels, was a chief suspect. His face might have held clues.

All it seemed to hold by the time I got into the kitchen, though, was the slight jitter of too much coffee—and shifting secrets. Both he and my grandmother stopped talking when I came in, and I had the distinct idea they had been having a conversation about *me.*

We traded Good Mornings. At the GGCF it was very important to greet people properly and say good-bye properly if you didn't want to lose cake privileges.

"Well, Ella," my grandmother said, after a minute of watching me pour pieces of bark into a bowl. (I hadn't talked her into the Cheerios school of grocery shopping.) "Christopher and I were just having a discussion."

"Mmm hmm." I tried to sound polite, with my mouth full of fiber.

"And he asked me an interesting question." She was watching me intently. Like a hawk, in fact. "He wondered why you and Rosie were *outside* when the alarm went off last night. I was too flustered to notice, but Christopher pointed out that when you came in through the front door, Rosie was with you."

Thanks, Abercrombie.

"What were you doing up?" she asked.

I swallowed. "Rosie couldn't sleep," I explained. "She knocked on the door outside my room. But the door was stuck, so I had to walk all the way around."

"So that's why you came galumphing through my bedroom in the small hours," Abercrombie commented. *Galumphing*: how rude. I was being so quiet!

"Wasn't that rather unusual—for Rosie to come talk to you in the night like that?" the GM asked.

Well, yes, it was, of course. But I suddenly worried about mentioning that Miguel hadn't been in the cabin. I didn't want to get him into trouble.

"I was trying to be nice," I said. "She seemed—upset."

That didn't sound too good either, though.

"I see." My grandmother looked at Abercrombie, her eyebrows raised. He raised his in reply. It was like a code—the eyebrow code. "And was Miguel with you girls?"

I kept chewing, to give myself time. "I think Miguel was

already looking for the—uh—intruder," I finally said. "That's why Rosie was upset. She was scared, for her dad."

Abercrombie Books was looking right at me. From his unfriendly gray eyes I knew he thought I was lying. I wondered if he thought *I* had done it: that I had taken Kepler's *Dream* or had something to do with taking it. Was Our Honored Pest going to try to persuade my own grandmother that I was a criminal?

She cleared her throat. "As you know, Ella, this theft is a very serious matter."

"I know."

"It is not some sort of amusing joke."

"Right." Was I laughing? No, I was not. There was nothing funny about the fact that the guy with the goatee was trying to frame me.

"And today, to explore one possible explanation, or at least to have a better sense of what happened, Christopher and I are going to talk to—Tweedle—that is—"

"Jackson and Jason?" I suggested.

"Indeed. We are going to see whether they can shine any light on the situation."

"But if you think you saw anything last night that might explain what happened, Ella," Abercrombie put in, oilily, "it would be helpful if you told us."

I was thinking, *"Us"? Get this guy out of the room, lady, and then I'll talk.* Though all I would have been able to confess was that yes, I had smuggled Froot Loops and one, ahem, *borrowed* photograph into my room, and played the occasional mindless game of Jewel Quest. None of which would have advanced our case against the thief of Kepler's *Dream*.

There was a shuffling at the door, Hildy started yapping again, just in case we'd been missing the sound, and before I knew what had hit us, there was an outbreak of teenagers right there in the kitchen. Tweedledum and Tweedledee appeared, the tall one chewing on a seed or two as usual and the other one, phone-less, looking incredibly uncomfortable, like he had no idea what to do with his thumbs. For lack of a better option, he had them hooked into his jeans pockets.

Grandmother greeted them, and they grunted and nodded in reply. Usually that wouldn't be good enough for her, but I guess the rules for workers at the facility were more lax than for us inmates.

"How's it going, Uncle C?" Textless said to Abercrombie.

"Well enough, thank you, Jason," he replied. "Are you getting ready for the holiday?"

More nods and grunts. *Uncle C?* I looked back and forth between Jason, the texter, and Mr. Books, and now I could see the resemblance. Yes, they were related. That did suddenly explain something about how he got a job with the GM. But then that also might mean that Jason had *aided* his uncle, like they say in detective stories, in the heist.

"Something has happened, boys," the GM announced, "that we need to discuss."

"Yes, Violet," Mr. Books said. He looked over at me like I was a TV channel that needed to be changed. Switched off, even. "But first, shouldn't we—er—?"

"Ah, yes." She nodded. "Ella: after last night's commotion, I felt it would be a good day for you to be occupied elsewhere, so earlier this morning I made a telephone call. Carlos Aguilar has kindly offered to give you a riding lesson in about an hour."

Well, I wasn't going to say no to that. It was a little hard to see how I was going to combine my new detective career with my ambitions to become a cowgirl, but maybe, I figured, there was a way to be both at once. *Ella Mackenzie, the Galloping Gumshoe. She solves in the saddle. She guesses while she gallops . . .*

It was clear I was supposed to disappear, so I took Lou outside for a walk. I wandered around in my now slightly scuffed boots, and then saw something very strange: a bright blue peacock the size of an ostrich half hiding behind the feed bins.

Only it wasn't a peacock. It was Rosie. She stood up when she saw me. "Oh," she said, trying to act casual. She popped a pink bubble. "Hi."

I looked at her. I didn't want to be rude, but, "Um—what are you doing?"

She seemed only a little embarrassed. "I was just"—she lowered her voice to a whisper as she brushed the dirt from her hands—"trying to listen."

To the feed bins? The birds? "To what?" I asked.

"Those guys. Those slobby guys. Who are they?"

"You mean Jason and Jackson?" I decided not to confuse her,

so I gave the right names. "They're these two high school seniors who are helping my grandmother out in her library. They work for her."

"They work for her? Seriously?"

"That's the idea. I guess they know a lot about computers."

"That part I can believe." Rosie shook her head. Her hair was back in its neat riding braid down her back. "But, I don't like to say this—well, they don't talk about your grandmother with a lot of respect."

"Really?"

She told me how she had heard Tweedledum and Tweedledee out in the driveway joking about "the Stern One" and her "Labyrinth of Books," and then how one of them—the short one, she said, who by now I knew was Jason, Abercrombie's relation—made some crack in a low voice that made the other guy explode with a loud, laughing . . . expletive.

I explained to Rosie about "expletive deleted" and how handy it was around foulmouthed people. She thought that was funny. We started walking around the back tangle together with Lou, talking about teens—how when some people turn sixteen they suddenly seem to stop doing anything but swearing and texting. I told Rosie about the day in Santa Rosa when there was an obnoxious bunch of high schoolers on our bus ride home and Abbie had made up a new word: *meanagers*.

"I like that," Rosie said. "My cousin Lola can be a meanager sometimes." She ducked under a low-hanging branch. "Do you have cousins?"

"Two," I told her. "They're boys who live in Arizona and who only care about football."

Rosie rolled her eyes, like, Enough said. By now we had circled around and were back in the driveway. Rosie stopped and looked at me. "Ella," she said. "I want to figure out who took your grandmother's book."

This surprised me. Why should she care? I couldn't think of a polite way to ask, but Rosie answered anyway. "If I don't figure it out, people might think my dad, or someone he's connected to, had something to do with it. So—"

"Abercrombie," I interrupted her. "He's the only one who would think that. My grandmother wouldn't."

She shrugged, and suddenly I felt an awkwardness between us.

"Well, anyway," I said, "I want to figure it out, too. I think it *was* Abercrombie, and I think he's a creep and my grandmother doesn't realize it."

So that was how Rosie and I decided, kicking around the dust while we waited for Miguel, to go into business together as the Aguilar and Mackenzie Agency. We were jazzed about it, until Miguel came out to drive us to the Circle C.

He looked distracted. Not exactly unfriendly—Miguel was always kind, whether you were a person, a pooch or a peacock. He just wasn't a hundred percent *there* in the truck with Rosie and me. A piece of him was somewhere else. The way a piece of me drifted off to Seattle to be with my mom when the GM was telling me about her travels in Haiti, or why she hated the way I used the word *like* as a filler.

As the truck crossed the Rio Grande, I said, "There she is, the mighty river," hoping to get some kind of laugh at the sight of that rusty brown soup, but Rosie just looked away, and Miguel said "Uh-huh," like he wasn't even listening.

Once we got to the Circle C, though, none of that mattered, because for an hour at least I only thought about horses. Getting good at riding turned out to have a lot to do with your butt. Sure, the reins were important, but Carlos said that what marked a true cowgirl from someone slopping around like a kid at a pony ride (I blushed) was having their butt in the right place and communicating with their legs. "Don't tell your horse one thing with your legs and something else with your reins—that'll only confuse 'em. That's like your mom telling you not to eat candy and your dad saying it's fine." He winked, and I realized Carlos didn't know my own dad never told me anything about what to eat, unless it was before a six a.m. fishing trip.

By the end of the lesson I wasn't quite ready to herd cattle or ride in a rodeo, but I was able to trot around the ring on Paloma without falling off. So when Rosie got back from her ride and asked, "How'd it go?"—this time without the snotty undertone, just interested—I could look her in the eye and say, "Not bad." Carlos bragged about how I definitely had cowgirl legs and before anyone knew it I'd be out on the mesa with the rest of my posse.

Miguel was gone, I noticed, and Carlos explained that he had errands to run and had suggested I stay on at the ranch that day. So I got to go into the big house with Rosie and Lola and have some of Tía Gloria's fantastic enchiladas. Mexican food, at last!

After lunch, Rosie offered to show me around the stables. We ambled through dirt and flies to a huge metal-sided building. Once inside, Rosie took me all up the long, cool central corridor, telling me which horse was which. "This is my boy, Mocha . . . and Juno, he's a frisky one . . . and Rocky . . . and Picchu . . ."

"Wait. What did you call that one?" I pointed at a smoky-gray pony.

"Picchu." Rosie half smiled, and kicked at some hay. "It's a goofy name, I gave it to her. It's short for Machu Picchu, which is a place in Peru."

"I know."

"They have these really amazing old ruins there, up on a mountaintop—"

"I know."

"—And one day I want to go."

"Me too."

Rosie finally stopped talking. "Really?" She squinted at me in that way cool girls do when they think you're just copying them. So I explained that my mom and I had talked about it, and about the Vacation Game we used to play, and how one night we read about Machu Picchu together and decided it would be a cool place to go.

"I think so too. My uncle Ignacio has been there." Rosie looked into Picchu's stable and saw the pony needed more oats, so she took a big bucket and went over to get more. As she was scooping oats, Rosie said, not quite facing me, "So I heard your mom is sick. And that's why you came out here."

"Yeah." My stomach, heavy with enchiladas, got even heavier. It was never easy to talk about this. "She's got leukemia. Which is, you know—cancer."

"Yeah."

"So she's being treated at a hospital in Seattle. They're giving her a stem cell transplant in a couple of days, on the Fourth. It's a pretty tough treatment, I guess, they blast them with radiation and stuff, so she thought it would be better if I did some kind of trip while she was doing it."

"Why didn't you just go stay with your dad?"

"Oh. Well, see—" How to explain the whole mess in one line? "It didn't work out." I shrugged.

Rosie nodded, like that was clear enough. She had filled the bucket, but before carrying it over to the pony she paused. She looked straight at me, her face open and serious.

"Is your mom going to die?"

Now, *die* was not a word people used around me. They found lots of other phrases—"I know your mom's going to pull through," "Amy's going to beat this thing," "one day this will all be a distant memory"—but it was always *that* kind, the kind about her getting better. If someone told you about their friend or relative who had had cancer, it always turned out that the person got cured and everything went back to normal. They never told you the other stories. The sad ones. The ones where all the medicine and operations *didn't* work.

No one, not even Dr. Lanner, wanted to admit that that happened, too.

"I don't know," I told Rosie. I swallowed. The enchiladas had become a gross mass of worry in the pit of my stomach. I was afraid I might be about to cough them back up. "I hope not." Which was probably pretty obvious.

Then Rosie did something interesting. She ran her fingers along the beads of her pretty necklace, her eyes closed. She murmured, as if she were talking to someone I couldn't see. Or as if she were praying.

She opened her eyes suddenly and I saw how brown they were, the color of the thick, strong coffee my mom used to drink every morning, before she got sick.

"She's going to get better," Rosie told me. Her face was kind, and sure. Suddenly I could see the resemblance between her and Miguel. "That's what my *abuelito* is telling me. She isn't going to die."

I wanted to hug Rosie, but I wasn't sure she'd want me to, so I just stroked the nose of the horse nearest me instead and asked, "Your *abuelito*?"

"My grandpa. He passed away a long time ago, but sometimes he tells me things, if I ask him. If they're important."

She acted like this was not an especially surprising thing. "That's cool," I said, which was lame, but I was trying to distract her from the fact that I was rubbing my eyes, in case tears threatened to pool. I pretended I had gotten some dust in there. Still: it *was* cool that Rosie could talk to her grandfather. I would have liked to be able to talk to Edward Mackenzie, too. Dead or alive. "I never knew mine," I said. "He died before I was even born."

"I know." She nodded. "Mine too."

"Oh, yeah?" I remembered something. "Hey. Didn't your grandfather used to work for my grandparents?" I felt weird about asking, but I was too curious not to.

"Yeah." She turned away to carry the oats back to Picchu, and I thought maybe she wanted me to change the subject. It made us seem unequal. Even if I didn't myself grow up with diamonds and peacocks and a million books everywhere, but just in a regular house in Santa Rosa with my optometrist mom, next door to a nice lady who liked watching old Bruce Lee movies.

It was cool and quiet when we got back later to the GGCF. Miguel and Rosie dropped me and then vanished. Hildy padded to the door, as if to warn me that her mistress was napping. Lou and I played outside for a while, but I think he could tell my heart wasn't in it.

"Ella? Is that you?" Framed by the blue doorway, just like when I saw her for the first time a hundred years ago—way back in June—was Violet Von Stern. She looked sleepy and strangely emptied, like a soccer ball that's lost air, or a pillow with half its feathers gone.

"Where have you been?" She peered at me in confusion.

"At the Circle C. Learning to ride." This was weird, her forgetting. It was like Mom on chemo. With my mom I had learned to stop saying, *Remember?* That only made her feel bad. ("It's bad enough to be bald and ugly," she said to me one day in May, "but it's especially unfair if I become an imbecile, too.")

The GM's blue eyes became clearer now. "Oh yes, of course.

The Circle C. So you were." She shook her head, as if to get the cobwebs out of it. "Come along, Brunhilda. Let's get some fresh air."

She walked slowly outside. "Christopher has gone off to do a bit of sightseeing in Old Town," she told me. "He's very upset about the Kepler disappearance. We both are." Her voice sounded heavy and tired. "We spent the entire morning searching the Library, in case the volume had somehow been misfiled, and trying to determine whether the boys knew anything about it. They did not." I decided to keep quiet. "And no, frankly, I don't think Tweedledum and Tweedledee would be capable of any sort of deeper conspiracy. Those boys have nothing upstairs." She looked at me. "I mean, Ella, there's very little furniture up there at all." Now she sounded more like herself. Pulling insults out again was waking her up. "Really, the whole notion of an actual, physical *book* is entirely foreign to those boys. Granted, they understand computers, but reading something between two covers, on printed pages, rather than on a screen? Completely exotic. I think those young men have found working in the Library akin to looking at cave drawings, or petroglyphs—exploring evidence of some earlier, primitive culture."

We had wandered over to the cratered area under the high cottonwoods where Hildy and Lou were sniffing around in bird poop together like old pals. You really have to be a dog, I guess, to appreciate bird poop fully.

"This used to be a pond, you know," the GM told me. "With

swans and ducks swimming about in it. When Edward was still alive."

"Yeah . . . Uh, *yes*. Miguel told me."

"Did he?" My grandmother seemed surprised. "I suppose he might remember, though he was young then. His brothers were older." She sighed. "Did Miguel tell you about the trees?" She gestured around us. I shook my head.

"Well, they were planted by Edward, years ago, when we first moved here. In the pattern of the Big Dipper. It was one of his wedding presents to me—a 'constellation of cottonwoods,' he called it. You can hardly tell now, but the pattern is still there." She looked up into the high trees, and some late-afternoon leaf light fell on her worn face. "I miss Edward, Ella. Even after all this time. I miss his conversation, his company, his sense of humor. I know it may seem strange, but that book—that single book—was one of my great connections to my late husband." She sighed. "It made me feel closer to him. That is why I will be heartbroken to lose Kepler's *Dream*. It's not just the value of the volume—not the monetary value, that is."

"I know what you mean," I said.

"Do you?"

"It's like something that represents the person when they're not around." I touched the bracelet on my wrist. The thing's importance wasn't something you could *see*. It was just some cheap metal. But I never took it off. "A kind of charm."

"That's exactly it." The GM looked at me with a new warmth in her eyes. "You know, my friend Joan thinks you're an exceptional girl, Ella. Uncommonly intelligent. And strong." It was as though she was seeing someone new in front of her. "She may be right."

This was, by a factor of about a thousand, the nicest thing Violet Von Stern had ever said about me. I took a deep breath. It was now or never.

"Grandmother, there's something I'd like to know," I said to her. "How did Edward die? What happened exactly, in the accident?"

The GM startled instinctively, like a phantom dog had just jumped up to bite her. Then I saw her try to settle herself. "He was fishing," she began slowly. "On the Rio Grande. With Walter." She paused, staring out at the emptied pond. "And Oscar, and Ignacio, too. Oscar Aguilar was—"

"—Rosie's grandpa," I supplied. Suddenly things that had been all blurry were beginning to go clear in my mind. Coming into focus.

"That's right." She nodded. "Oscar worked here for us. He was marvelous with the horses, the dogs, the birds—all the creatures. And his boys, Ignacio, Carlos and Miguel, were often about. They all played with Walter." I could almost see this group of kids reflected in the GM's deep blue eyes. "In any case, Oscar and Edward used to go out on fishing trips together. They liked to take the older boys, too—not around here, but upriver where the Rio Grande is deeper and broader. I was never happy when they were gone. I never understood the lure of fishing, pardon the pun, and I didn't like being left alone. I—I always had the feeling that something was going to go wrong." A dark, old sadness crossed my grandmother's face. "And one day, you see, it did."

She stared out at the dead pond, as if watching the ghosts of birds glide around it. Long-ago swans. Ducks of the old days. "It was hard to know exactly what happened. Walter was being a daredevil, I imagine, as he often was at that age. In any case, he was out in the river, or too close to it, and his father went in after him to pull him back to the bank. And then, a rogue current came . . ." Her voice caught. "The river took Edward, and he drowned."

"And Rosie's grandpa, too."

"Yes. Oscar, too. He must have followed, to try to help."

I remembered Miguel's comment the first time we crossed the Rio Grande. "Dangerous river," he had called it. I had found that hard to believe.

"So the boys lived, and the men died. The children could hardly speak afterwards, for days. They were in shock, of course. The police came to investigate, which was utterly pointless and rather lowered my opinion of the profession. As if they could be heroes by proving there had been some argument between Oscar and my husband. Fools." I was glad Officer Barker couldn't hear her opinion of the men in blue. "What happened that morning on the river was an accident. And a dreadful tragedy." My grandmother turned to walk back into the house. "It wasn't Walter's fault, I suppose, or Ignacio's. They were young, they meant no harm. And yet . . . " She shook her head. "I couldn't help feeling that if the children hadn't been there, the men might simply have caught their fish, and come home."

I remembered Miguel talking about his family moving away, and their getting rid of the horses. I wondered what had happened to my dad.

"Walter went away to school soon after that," my grandmother said, as if she had heard my question. "Boarding school. It seemed to be for the best."

I wasn't sure what to say. Watching your father drown, then being sent away to school: it was a lousy story. For maybe the first time in my life, I felt sorry for my dad. Maybe it hadn't been such a picnic for him, either.

"And ever since losing Edward, I've forced myself to be adventurous, to move out into the world. As a distraction, partly. I have thrown myself into my travels, and when I am here, I devote myself to the Library. As a way of feeling close to him, still."

I could see my grandmother snapping out of her trance now, and coming back to the present tense.

"So you see, Ella. It's given all of us rather too much history to carry around."

I realized something very strange. I was feeling sorry for her, too. For Violet Von Stern!

"I want to help you find it," I said to my grandmother. "Kepler's *Dream,* I mean. I want to help figure out who took it—and get it back."

She looked at me, her eyes deep and blue as a river or a sea.

"Thank you. It's a noble ambition." The GM shook her head, and there was some part of the story on her face I didn't think she'd ever tell, details she'd never shade in for me. "But I don't believe we will ever find Kepler's lovely *Dream*. Some things in life are lost"—her gaze wandered up into the trees for a moment—"and we never do find them again."

Dear Mom,

Well, today's the day for your new blood. It's funny they chose July Fourth—like the whole country is celebrating. I wonder if you can see fireworks from your room.

I keep thinking about you saying that the stuff they gave you looks like tomato juice. Now every time I open the fridge and see a bottle of Grandmother's V8, I'm going to feel queasy. I don't care how many vitamins and nutrients they put in there, I'm never going to drink it. What am I—a vampire?

A lot has been happening around here. Well, one especially bad thing: a book of Grandmother's got stolen. Not just any book, either. Her most important, fancy, and worth-a-lot-of-money book. The alarm went off in the middle of the night and she realized it was gone. The police came and everything, though no one was hurt. No one was caught, either.

The police said that because there was no sign of anyone forcing their way in, it is probably some kind of "inside job." Meaning: one of US! The other thing about the police is, they don't seem too worried about it. Grandmother wasn't very impressed by their grammar, either.

My own guess is that it was Mr. Books, in the Library, with a Knapsack. But unless I get any proof, all I can do is just that—guess. If it were a game of Clue, I could draw a few cards and figure it out that way (I'm sure it isn't Colonel Mustard, and for some reason it's never Professor Plum), but as it is, I guess I'm going to have to do real work. With Rosie. She is being nice to me now, by the way. It turns out maybe we will be friends after all. She likes horses, gum, spy movies and music. She used to think soccer was a waste of time until Mexico was in the World Cup, and now she admits it's a little bit—just a _little_ bit—cool.

Having Mr. Abercrombie around, though, is a pain in my saddle—a phrase I learned from Rosie's uncle Carlos. Thanks to him, Mr. Books, that is, the meals have gotten even worse—fish (gag!) and the other night, even liver (!!!). On the liver night I had to dip into the supplies Auntie Irene sent me for emergencies, which include beef jerky and also Froot Loops. I hope you're not mad about the Froot Loops. I know they are illegal in our house, but as Auntie Irene said, "Extreme Situations require Extreme Responses." The other day I thought of the chicken potpie you make and wondered when I will get to eat something that good again. But I guess food is probably the last thing on your mind.

Happy Independence Day.

I miss you.

I love you.

Ella

EIGHT

Abercrombie
and Snitch

Rosie decided she had better do her work in the background, where she wouldn't be seen. As a family member, even if the Mackenzie family was not exactly a model of togetherness, I could probably go into the more restricted zones. So, some days later, with Lou along as my beard—the "beard," I learned once from a movie, is the innocent guy who goes along with you as part of your disguise—I ambled over to the Librerery.

I wasn't expecting telltale fingerprints or spatters of blood or anything, but it couldn't hurt to take a look at the place again and try to imagine what could have happened that night while Rosie was shivering nervously out behind my room and I was wandering through the back tangle trying to find her.

I remembered hearing weird noises. Maybe they were just dreams or ghosts; then again, maybe they were the solid snobbish footsteps of Abercrombie Books. Could Our Honored Guest really have gotten to the Library and back during that time, so he could still come out of his room in his robe looking sleepy right after the alarm went off? Or had Mr. Books planted someone else—an accomplice, possibly a guy good with his thumbs—to rustle around in the books for him and shuffle off with the most valuable one in the collection?

And how would whoever it was have gotten into the Library anyway, unless, like that policeman said, the door had accidentally-on-purpose been left . . . open?

As I approached the steps down to the building that morning, I saw that the door was ajar, again. That surprised me: it seemed early in the day for Tweedledum and Tweedledee to be working. I told Lou to entertain himself digging up old skunk remains, tapped the door lightly, and there in the dimness saw Christopher Abercrombie. Counting. Counting and murmuring and counting and murmuring, looking all through my grandmother's many, many remaining books.

He was moving a finger along the edge of a far-off bookshelf when he saw me. He jumped, like he'd been caught with his hand in the cookie jar. A little revenge for the time he'd sneaked up on me while I was listening to the GM on the phone with my dad.

"Ella!" Abercrombie exclaimed. "What brings you here?" A pair of glasses dangled around his neck like jewelry. "I assumed you were one of the boys reporting for work. Not that they usually manage to get here at such a tender hour. I think they view mornings much as zombies do: not a time to be about."

I ignored his joke. Who had time for zombies? "I want to find out what happened to Kepler's *Dream.*" I looked right at him, doing my best evil eye. It was supposed to get him to confess right there and then. Or at least make his face develop a guilty twitch.

If there was a twitch, though, or a shadow of guilt, I missed it. All I saw was the familiar smirk.

"How marvelous," he said. "Young Ella to the rescue!"

I didn't see that sarcasm was necessary here.

"You share your grandmother's lack of faith in the Albuquerque Police Department, I take it?" I nodded. "So do I, I'm afraid."

Then Abercrombie peered at me closely, as though I were some kind of specimen. His goatee seemed to quiver. He looked a little like a goat, in fact.

"And tell me, Ella," he bleated, "what is your theory, currently?"

"Theory?"

"Yes. Who do *you* suppose would take the trouble to break in to your grandmother's library to steal a rare, valuable edition of a work of astronomy?"

"Well . . ." I wasn't expecting this question. I wasn't in the mood to chitchat with Abercrombie about what I supposed.

"A precocious adolescent from the nearby Juvenile Facility? Who has long wanted to read Kepler's posthumous masterpiece?"

The thought of those trapped teenagers had crossed my mind, but he was right, it did seem far-fetched.

"Or perhaps a little magpie flew into the Library, drawn by the glitter of the genuine gold leaf on the pages?"

I swear, he winked at me.

"Who would even know enough about this book to steal it?"

I shrugged. He was making me nervous, the way he was watching me. "Well, it seems like . . ."

I hesitated. He nodded, with that (expletive deleted) smile on his face.

"Ye-e-e-s?" he pressed. "It seems like . . . ?"

It seemed like Abercrombie Books was more of a pain than ever. It seemed like he was messing with me to throw me off the scent. I needed Lou in there—he might not have been a blood-hound, but he had a better nose than I did.

"It seems like . . . It probably wasn't a stranger," I said finally.

"That's right!" Abercrombie clapped, like a teacher trying to lead me to the right answer. "But what, Ella," he went on—and I started, for the first time ever, to wish those high school boys would show up, to spare me more of this conversation—"would someone even plan to do with this book, once they had it?"

This at least seemed obvious. "Sell it."

"Ah, but you see"—Abercrombie Books was now exception-ally pleased with himself—"a *Morris* Kepler, a Morris edition of the famous *Somnium,* or *Dream,* though one of the most sought-after volumes among bibliophiles, would be"—he looked at me pointedly—"*impossible to sell* out in the world. Each of the extraordinarily few extant copies is accounted for. Which, paradoxically, makes a stolen volume at once invaluable—and worthless."

I folded my arms.

"But I fear that whoever ran off with Kepler's *Dream* might not be aware of that. Which means they may be in for a ter-rible shock." He gave a hearty, fake chuckle, as if that idea was hilarious. "Here, Ella," he continued in a hushed tone. "Let me show you something I discovered earlier, may I?"

And he ushered us both to the end of the room, where the books were deep in shadow. He was gesturing at something. At first I thought it was those glass shelves I hadn't looked at for a while, the ones with the medals, the fishing flies and the photos. The silvered man and his wife, when they were younger.

Then I realized Mr. Books was pointing at the fireplace.

"Isn't that surprising?"

All I saw was ashes. What was so surprising about that? It was a fireplace. I hated him thinking he was so smart, though, so I stared for a minute—and suddenly my brain caught up with me. *Ashes*. Who had been burning a fire in there?

"Your grandmother doesn't often visit the Library in the evening, does she?" Abercrombie knew she didn't. "I wonder who else might have come into the Library and lit a fire."

He bugged his eyes out dramatically, and I couldn't tell if he thought *I* had. I had built a fire only once in my life: the night the book disappeared, when Rosie and I were in Miguel's cabin trying to get warm. But there was no way Abercrombie could know about that.

"I'll tell you what I have noticed, Ella," he continued in a confiding tone, like suddenly I was his best friend. "I've noticed that Miguel Aguilar makes most of the fires around this place. Have you noticed that? He's very skilled at it."

I glared at him, my arms still folded. I knew what Abercrombie was suggesting—that Rosie's dad had something to do with taking the *Dream*—and like Rosie, I knew it was ridiculous. But we were going to have to find a way to prove something different.

There was a rustle outside.

Abercrombie raised his eyebrows. "It's one of the zombies," he stage whispered. Really, the guy should have been in the theater, not in books.

It was the short one who came inside, and though he had yet to make eye contact with me that summer, for once I was really glad to see his Texty self. Plus, for the first time ever he seemed wide awake and like he had something on his mind.

"Top of the morning to you, Jason!" Abercrombie's nephew rolled his bleary eyes as he swung his backpack off his shoulder. "What brings you in so early this morning? Shouldn't you be—"

"That (expletive deleted)," Texty interrupted. He jerked his head backward, like a peacock, at some invisible figure behind him. "That should be his name, Jack (expletive deleted), not Jack*son*."

"Jason—please. The child!" Abercrombie chided. *Child!* That again. What was I, in elementary school still? Besides, I was used to expletives. I guess Abercrombie didn't know my dad.

For the first time in history, Jason looked at me. He shrugged. "So-rry," he said, with as much sincerity as a kid who's been caught eating candy. "Listen, I've got to talk to you, Uncle C. Something super-important."

"Well, carry on, I'm just here taking note of a few catalog items . . ."

"Yeah, but it shouldn't be in front of *the child*." He imitated his uncle's drawl, and I had a minute of wanting to sic Lou on Jason, to nip his busy little thumbs.

The two of them traded looks for a moment, goaty uncle to texty teenager, and then decided to go off to take a walk, leaving me there on my own.

I didn't mind that. It was the first time I had been in the *Librery* by myself, and it was a peaceful place. My grandmother's church of books.

I went over to the shelves that had always interested me the most and found the photographs of my grandfather. A man who had known the stars. The real stars in the sky, but also the stars I used to worship, the way some kids do celebrities: Aldrin, Armstrong, Collins. I stared at his silvered face and wished it could speak to me.

"Ah, Ella. Here you are." The silvery lady from one of those frames, now older, appeared in the room. I was worried I might get in trouble for being in there alone, without any white gloves on, but my grandmother seemed distracted.

"I am going off for a hair appointment today. I may as well look my best, today of all days," she said, the last part under her breath. "And after that I had thought of lunching at Chez Albertine, to cheer myself up." She looked like she needed cheering. "Would you care to come along?"

I guess I must have had a long face, as Mom used to call it. ("Ella, sweetie, don't give me one of your long faces. It makes you look too much like Lou.") "Perhaps you don't care for the idea," my grandmother said. She tried to sound light, but her eyes were disappointed.

"Well," I said, fumbling around for an excuse, "I was planning to hang out with—that is, talk with . . ." I doubted *hang out* was on the slang menu I was supposed to use.

"Your friend who chews gum?" She meant Rosie, of course. "Would you like to ask her to join us?"

Now, I may have a pretty good imagination—Ms. Nelson always told me I did when we did creative writing—but I couldn't picture Rosie and me and my grandmother all eating frogs' legs together. Or snails. Or even just steak and fries.

Luckily, the GM seemed to have the same thought. We looked at each other without saying anything, and I shivered. There it was: a family tie, after all. I knew what my grandmother was thinking, and she knew what I was thinking, and we didn't actually have to spell it out for each other in words at all.

"Or perhaps you and she would rather stay together and have lunch here," the GM said in as close to a nice voice as I'd heard her use with anyone other than Hildy. "I'm sure there must be some sandwich ingredients you could forage for in the pantry."

I nodded gratefully. "That would be great, Grandmother. Thanks."

"All right. Come out with me now, so I can lock up. Even if it is an instance of shutting the barn door once the horse has gone." She gazed back over her shoulder as we left. "I am glad you were looking at the photographs of Edward," she said. "This is an important day to remember him, Ella. Every day is, of course, but—today in particular."

"Why?"

"July seventh," she said, "is the day he died."

I couldn't think of the right response to that news, so I just stayed quiet. No wonder she was so sad, though. In a minute, she was climbing slowly into her giant white car, and with a tired wave, she drove away.

Leaving me to find my friend who chewed gum.

The person who materialized out of the dust, like someone in a sci-fi movie, wasn't Rosie, though. It was Tweedledum (unless it was Tweedledee). Jackson, the tall, thin one, who was an (expletive), according to Abercrombie's nephew. He was wandering over from the direction of the back tangle, his head full of whatever fills a high-schooler's head.

He reached instinctively for a few sunflower seeds in his pocket and popped them into his mouth. "Hey," he mumbled through the shells, which was maybe the first word he had ever spoken to me directly.

"Hey," I replied. "What's up?"

Then I realized that this was one of my suspects and I really ought to interrogate him, as a good detective would.

This was how it went:

Me: So, um, how's it going, working for my grandmother?

(Trying to put the suspect at ease, as if it is easy to put a meanager at ease.)

Him: It's OK.

(*No immediate sign of guilt, just a general spaciness.*)

Me: She's pretty upset about that Kepler book being taken.

Him: I know, yeah.

Me: It was a pretty cool book. All about life on the moon.

Him: Uh-huh. (*Slight shiftiness here, like the look Lou has when there's a plate of salami on the kitchen counter and you're pretty sure the stack has lost a few slices.*)

Me: It's not like whoever took it is going to be able to sell it.

Him: I know, I know. Mr. Abercrombie already explained all that to us.

Me: Oh. (*So much for the investigator's effort to act knowledgeable.*)

Him: Which is why I think Jason should have just *chilled* about the whole thing. Chill out, dude! (*For some reason, this random exclamation made the suspect laugh.*) He should have figured that out.

Me: There he is now. He's not looking too chilled.

(*Spotting Suspect No. 2 coming up the path, looking pretty grumpy.*)

Him: No kidding.

This interview didn't seem to be getting us very far. I guess I couldn't cross the middle-school/teenager divide after all. Tweedledee (or was it Tweedledum?)—Jason, in the distance—didn't seem eager to be part of our party, and I wasn't about to push my luck with him right now. I figured I had just better find

Rosie. I gave the suspect a parting compliment, though, in case it softened him up.

Me: I like your T-shirt. *(It was the one that said POLARIS: FIND YOUR TRUE NORTH.)*

Him: Thanks. *(For a second as though noticing me as an actual human being.)* Everyone has to find theirs, you know.

Me *(with no idea what this meant, but not wanting to seem like an idiot)*: Yeah. Definitely!

Him: Later.

Me: OK.

And I wandered off to the back tangle to look for Rosie, leaving the tall boy to gaze at the trees and chew his sunflower seeds, sharing the shells with the grateful peacocks.

It wasn't the best morning's work I've ever done. Let's just say I've had spelling tests that went better. I wasn't ready, as Encyclopedia Brown would have been by then, to close my eyes for two minutes and come up with the story of who took the Morris Kepler, and where the book was now, and why. There were plenty of mysteries: the ashes in the fireplace, the Abercrombie Books angle, the unknown argument between Tweedledum and Tweedledee. My brain hurt trying to figure it all out.

I had gone rootling around in the bushes back behind my bedroom, trying to figure out where Rosie had gotten to, when I heard a voice calling me from somewhere above.

"Helloooooo, Ella!"

"Rosie?"

"Hellooooooooo."

It really seemed like her voice was coming from above my head. What was she, an angel all of a sudden?

"Where are you?" I craned my head back to gaze up into the cottonwood trees. All I could see were the long, bright green tail feathers of some of the birds.

Suddenly I saw a face. A laughing face. Near the edge of the roof.

"Up here!"

She gave a little wave.

"How did you get up there?"

"Shhhhh! I'll show you." And she stood up and walked along the edge of the flat adobe surface. She gestured for me to follow her, so I did, along the ground, until she led me around to a place in the back where one of the smaller trees, not a cottonwood but some smaller, thicker-limbed tree, grew up close to the side of the house. "You just climb up there," she said, pointing. "And then onto the roof from that branch."

She made it sound so easy. It was a good climbing tree, though. It had a nice rough bark that made it easier to hold on. I swung up onto a low branch, and then monkeylike made my way through the branches, over, and on up.

"Hi!" Rosie said to me when I landed.

"Hi!" We high-fived.

I couldn't believe I'd been at my grandmother's this long and hadn't figured out that you could get onto the roof. I would have to include that on the house plan I had started drawing.

It was so cool up there: you could see the whole shape of the land and buildings around the House of Mud, the freeways not far off, and the Sandia Mountains in the distance. It was like being able to see ahead into your future—you got a sense of the whole master plan. There were a few peacocks nearby who weren't thrilled to be sharing the space with us, but they didn't make a racket about it. No more than usual, anyway.

"This is excellent," I said.

"Yeah," said my business partner. "It makes a great place to spy from." She looked at me. "So—any clues on the Killer Dolphin?"

We had decided it might be a good idea to come up with a code name for the stolen book, and she had come up with Killer Dolphin. Same initials.

"Nada," I reported. "Just some little spat between the two boys and a weird talk with Jackson. How about you?"

So then Rosie told me what she had heard.

She had staked herself out there, up on the roof, for much of the morning. Nothing much was happening, but she said she wanted to figure out where the thief might have gone when he or she left the Library. It was easier to get a sense of that with the aerial view.

I was impressed. There I had been, trying to get someone to confess, with zero results. Rosie was the one making lofty discoveries while I had been busy at ground level. I guess that was what you'd expect from a soccer player, keeping my feet on the ground.

After a while, she heard something. It sounded like Abercrombie, so she ducked down to be out of his sight line. He was pacing around the back of the property, talking with someone in a low voice. He must have figured they wouldn't be seen or overheard.

He hadn't taken into consideration the possibility of someone on the roof.

The problem with the exchange was that although Rosie could hear Abercrombie pretty clearly, the other one was a mumbler.

"Jason!" I told her. "It was Jason he was talking to. His nephew." I began to see what was irritating about mumblers: how could you eavesdrop on people if they didn't enunciate properly?

"Yeah, Jason. I thought so. So Abercrombie begins by saying, 'Now what did you need to talk to me about?'" Rosie did a pretty good Abercrombie imitation: she had his "I'm so important" tone down just right. She made her face kind of snooty as she spoke his lines. She'd probably end up in Drama Club one day. "And the answer was *mumble mumble mumble.* 'Good Lord, Jason, what *do* you mean? You're not suggesting—' Then the boy, Jason, mumbled some more. Abercrombie started huffing. 'Are you really suggesting that you would—' More mumbling. 'Well, I think Jackson was quite right to say that. After all, Mrs. Von Stern has been very generous. And you have *no* idea—' Then Jason must have started to get impatient, because his voice finally picked up, and I definitely heard him say, '. . . ripped you off, remember? At least that's what you told me,' and then his uncle goes, but in a lower voice, 'Yes, that's true, but it was long ago, and besides that was Edward, not Violet. In any case, please leave that worry to me. I have been working on another—'"

Rosie broke off.

"What?" I asked. "What? Working on another what?"

Her eyes got wide with frustration. "I don't *know*! Because then I heard some kind of weird creaky sound, like something opening, and then I heard Jason, crystal clear all of a sudden, SWEAR super-loudly—"

"That's meanagers for you."

"I know, and Abercrombie says, 'For heaven's sake, what is it?' and then Jason goes into some *very* quick mumble, then Abercrombie goes, 'I didn't think you were serious!' and at that point . . ."

At that point, Rosie had decided she had to try to see for herself what was happening, so she tried to inch closer to the edge of the roof to take a look. As she did that, though, a peacock standing not far from her started making one of those loud crying sounds, which startled her, and her foot slipped, sending a small pile of dead leaves and guano—which is bird poop, if you haven't read enough Tintin lately to know—over the edge of the roof.

"What the (expletive deleted)?" Abercrombie shouted. Not being a dog, he wasn't too fond of the stuff. "Who's there?"

Rosie had held her breath and lain absolutely flat. She said she asked her *abuelito* to keep the peacocks quiet for a minute, and it must have worked, because they shut up. Then she heard rapid footsteps, and she figured that though Abercrombie wanted to know if someone was watching them, he wanted to get them out of there even more.

And that was it.

Rosie stared at me in the bright noon Albuquerque sun. It was getting hot up there. "So? What do you think?" she asked me.

"I think we had better keep a very close eye on Christopher Abercrombie."

"Me too," she agreed. "And Jason. Didn't you say Abercrombie's leaving soon?"

"In a few days."

"We have to find a way to see if he's got it. You know, hidden in his bags or something."

So we started working on a plan of how to do that—stage an accidental-on-purpose search of Abercrombie's luggage. Then something surprising happened.

My cell phone rang. "Nowhere Man."

Nowhere Man hadn't called me for quite a while.

I hadn't even remembered I had the phone on me, it rang so little. But ever since Mom had the tomato juice put in her, I wanted to have the device nearby, just in case Auntie Irene ever needed to call me. For any reason.

"Dad?" I said, giving Rosie a *What do you know?* look. I had told her how flaky my dad was, how he had promised he would come to the GM's while I was staying here. And how he hadn't made it yet.

"Belle, old girl!"

Same greeting as usual, but he didn't sound quite as hearty as he sometimes did. There was a lot of static on the line.

"Hi."

"How's the crxxxxZcrsxxxx? Still crcxxxZing?"

"Where are you, Dad? Out on a raft somewhere? I can hardly hear you."

"Oh. Yeah, that's probably because I'm crxxxxZZxxxxZ."

This seemed so typical: by the time my dad was finally trying to call me, he wasn't even somewhere where he had a decent signal. I decided to lay—ahem! *lie*—flat on my back on the roof, soaking up some sun. There was some ratty old cloth up there, conveniently nearby, so I used that as a grimy sort of pillow and settled down.

"Uh-huh," I said into the phone, like I had any idea what he had just said.

"CrxxxxZZZxxxx July seventh," he said.

"Yeah." I was glad my dad was keeping track of the calendar. There were a few other things he was letting slide, like worrying about his daughter, but—whatever.

"CrxxxxZxxx crZxxxxxxZ Crxxx," he added. But then finally he came clear. "So she's probably going to the cemetery."

"Wait, what?" I asked him, sitting up. "What about the cemetery?"

"Mother usually goes there on the anniversary of my father's death. Today. I had thought of CrxxxxZxxx, but CRxxxxrzz ZZZZcxx."

"Oh. Right." I thought about my grandmother saying she was

getting her hair done that day. The idea that she wanted to look her best for a visit to the cemetery gave me a shudder of sadness. It wasn't as though Edward could still see her.

Rosie touched my arm and pointed to the tree, like she was going to climb back down. I nodded, and mouthed that I'd come in a sec.

"OK, Dad," I said, as if we had been having something like a real conversation. "So, you know, thanks for calling. Let me guess: you're not coming to visit, right?"

I don't know why I put it that way. It only made it easier for him—he hated having to admit he was bailing out on me. But it seemed stupid at this point to guess otherwise.

"Well, listen, Ella, that's one of the reasons I CrxxxxZxxx. You see, ZZxxxxCRxxxxx . . ."

Then I lost him. Or he lost me.

Either way, he was gone.

Dear Mom,

How are you doing? Auntie Irene said All Systems Are Go, according to the doctors, though they have to watch out that your old host blood doesn't fight with your new guest blood. I remember Dr. Lanner saying that could sometimes be a problem.

On playdates, though, you always taught me to make the guest feel welcome, like I would want to feel if I were at the other person's house. Remember? So I hope you're doing the same thing. Besides, if Violet Von Stern and I can find a way to get along, you and your tomato juice blood should be able to, too.

Auntie Irene told me something else that shocked me. That it's Aunt Miranda who donated the blood for your operation! Or the stems, or whatever it is exactly. Anyway, that as your sister, even if she has a totally different personality, she had just the right "match." Auntie Irene worried after it came out that she wasn't supposed to tell me. ("Oh, hell's bells!" she said, which is a funny one: what do hell's bells sound like? And how does anybody know?) She thought maybe you didn't want me to be mad at Aunt Miranda if the operation didn't work.

One thing I've been thinking about here at Broken Family Camp (another name I came up with) is when blood ties are important and when they're not. On the one hand, look at Auntie Irene, how much she's done for us, or Miguel, ditto, though they're not related to us by blood. On the other hand, look at Grandmother and Dad, who can barely have a telephone conversation without the phone bursting into flames. And now on the third hand—or maybe it's Lou's paws I should be counting on, so there are enough—Aunt Miranda has come through with a perfect match for you, and her blood will, we hope, get the job done.

I am still missing you a lot. I know on the phone you said you aren't very pretty right now, but guess what? I don't care! I'm not very pretty, either. I may not have been nuked, but my hair is halfway grown out and I look like a mutant. I'm seriously relieved no one at school can see it. That's one thing about summer: you can get through a bad haircut without comment from Caitlin Berenson or Chelsea Nash. Lou is, of course, too polite to mention it.

Pretty soon now I can come and visit you. Two weeks. I've got July 24th circled on the calendar in gold sparkly pen, with stars and stripes all around it.

Sometimes before I go to sleep, I get everything all mixed up—you being like an astronaut on your stem cell mission, and the host versus guest blood, and Grandmother's missing _Dream_. I forget who's going to the moon exactly, Kepler or Neil Armstrong or you. Whoever it is, my wish is still the same, that the return journey goes smoothly and after it's over we can all celebrate: MISSION ACCOMPLISHED!

I love you.

Ella

casa de
Estrellas

"HELLO?"

It was a tiny, scratchy voice—like one you would hear on some old-timey recording.

"Mo—*Mom*?"

I wasn't a stutterer, but it just didn't seem as though it could be her.

"Hi, sweetie."

It sounded as though my mom was speaking through the wrong end of a microphone, that instead of making her sound louder, shrank her right down to practically nothing.

"I won't talk long," I said. Auntie Irene, who was there visiting, had told me it was best to keep our conversations short, because Mom was really wiped out by all the treatment, but the truth was, it also spooked me to hear her. "I just wanted to say hello. So, you know: uh, hello!"

There was a silence, and then in the same scratchy voice from far away: "Did you find your dream?" I was pretty sure she said "dream," but it was hard to make out.

"You mean—Grandmother's book? No, we haven't found it yet. We're still trying to figure it out—"

"That dream. That . . . argument. All those years . . ." Mom's voice seemed to drift, and I wondered if she was going into one of her chemo moments. This nice nurse Faye in Seattle had told me that it was common for patients at this stage to get confused, and that if my mom said something I didn't understand, that was probably why.

"It's OK, Mom. It's just—it's an important book for Grandmother, and it's gone missing. But I'm all right. And I'll see you soon, OK? I'll be coming to visit soon."

I hated having to talk to her like she was a kid or from a foreign country or something. Auntie Irene got back on the line and I think she heard my voice wavering, like a kite in the wind, so she went straight into the Giants and how they were doing, to change the subject. I turned my charm bracelet around my wrist—*star, heart, bunny*—while Irene talked about the Giants' great pitchers and their cute rookie catcher.

And then I hung up. I wasn't feeling great after that. I could have gone for a quick shot of Jewel Quest, or even Boggle, but when I wandered over toward the kitchen, Abercrombie and the GM seemed to be huddled around the table having a heart-to-heart talk. Assuming they both had hearts—something I had only lately started to believe about my grandmother. The jury was still out on him.

Abercrombie was leaving at last, to go back and bother the Canadians. I'd be glad to see the back of him (another choice insult I got from the GM). In fact, I was staring at his back right then as he had his last breakfast at the Facility. I did envy him returning to the land of pancakes and bacon, though.

"Violet, I think given what has happened these past weeks, it makes sense," Abercrombie was saying in a hushed tone, "while you're traveling. For your peace of mind."

I hovered in the doorway, listening.

"Perhaps you're right." Grandmother sighed. "But it's a lot to ask of you, Christopher."

"You're not asking." His voice had a Splenda sweetness to it. (Those fake sweeteners: my mom hated them.) "I'm offering."

"You would be willing to do that? And you could afford more time away from the bookstore?"

"My assistant can manage ably."

My eyes got wider. I began to get an idea of what they were discussing.

"And you see, while I was here, I could bring the boys back—er, at least Jason—and together we could make real progress establishing the inventory. Making sure that the property—and the Library—were not unguarded in your absence."

(Expletive deleted)! She was thinking of letting the man stay there while she was on her next trip!

"Well, that's very kind of you." *Don't say yes!* It would be like letting the Big Bad Wolf babysit Little Red Riding Hood. Not a good plan. "But perhaps I simply shouldn't go away at all."

"Nonsense, Violet!" chided Our Honored Pest. "You love to travel. Besides, the South American trip sounds so . . . exotic."

"It does," she agreed. "But you see, Christopher, perhaps someone—that *same person*—is just waiting for me to leave, in order to ransack the place for other items."

There was a silence. Three busy brains were probably imagining who that person might be.

"It's so distressing," Abercrombie murmured. "But it's often the way: those people closest to home . . . in whom one has entrusted so much . . ."

"Yes. Close to home . . . ," my grandmother said, but I had the idea her thoughts were following their own direction, not Abercrombie's evil hint. I knew he was referring to Miguel, just like he had the other day when we were in the Librerery. The idea infuriated me. Miguel wasn't the creep around here. Look in the mirror, Abercrombie. There's the guy!

"Ahem!" I said from the kitchen doorway, so they wouldn't think I had been eavesdropping. I sounded alarmingly like Violet Von Stern.

"Ah, Ella," said the GM loudly. If I ever had to write up this House of Mud adventure—you know how at the beginning of the year in grade school, they make you write What I Did During My Summer Vacation—that's what mine could be called. *Ah, Ella.*

Abercrombie nodded primly. He'd be glad to see the back of me, too, I was pretty sure. "Can we help you?" he said, his forked tongue slipping out of his mouth for a moment.

"Actually, I was wondering if I could help *you*." I made my face all perky. "I thought I could help you with your bags. I guess you must be pretty beat after all your hours in the Library." Because it's such very *hard work* to pick up a book and shelve it.

"Well—surely—" Abercrombie was caught off guard. "That is, won't Miguel—"

"Miguel," I said pointedly, "is out running an errand for Grandmother." *Helping her out. Like he always does.*

"That's thoughtful of you, Ella," the GM weighed in. "I like seeing a willingness to be of help."

"Fine!" I said cheerfully, and trotted off to the Haitian Room before anyone could stop me.

The idea was to try to get a quick rummage around in there before Our Honored Pest chased after me. Rosie and I had decided it was our last, best option. I knew Abercrombie would be right behind me, but also that it wouldn't look good if he immediately got up from the table. I figured I had about a minute before he came in.

By now I was sure that Abercrombie had the Killer Dolphin and planned to whisk it back with him to Vancouver. He had found it that day when Rosie was on the roof and had been hiding it ever since. I could never forget the drooling expression on his face when we first talked about the Kepler book the day he arrived: my theory was that the minute he sold it to my grandmother, he wished he could get it back.

This was my chance to prove it.

Abercrombie's bags were on his bed. The carry-on—black leather, like a spy's briefcase—was open, so I slipped my hand in. All I could feel were pills, magazines and a laptop, but nothing the size of the Killer Dolphin. The KD was not a tiny book. You'd have to work to hide it, maybe conceal it inside something else. (I'm sure James Bond could come up with something.) If Abercrombie was taking the Dolphin with him, it must be in his suitcase.

I was wondering whether to risk unlocking that one when in he came, looking flustered.

"Ella, it's really not necessary—"

"No, no, that's all right!" I said in a loud, bossy voice. I felt more like my grandmother every minute. It was kind of fun.

Then I had a moment of inspiration. Abercrombie thought I *galumphed,* did he? Thought I was clumsy? Well, then it wouldn't surprise him if—

"Let me just carry this out for you," I offered, awkwardly hauling the suitcase down off the bed. As I did it, I managed to unfasten the lock so it fell open, and the case vomited its contents all over the floor.

"(Expletive deleted)!" shouted Abercrombie.

"Oh my gosh, I am *so* sorry!" I said, with about as much sincerity as someone who has just stopped you from scoring a goal by fouling you. "Here, let me—"

Pretending to help him, I started to put stuff back in his suitcase, while really of course I was looking around for the hollowed-out encyclopedia, or Kepler's *Dream* wrapped up in a purple bathrobe.

But nothing was that size and weight. I saw souvenirs placed around his clothes—a string of chili pepper lights, a bottle of hot sauce, a Navajo blanket. There was even one ratty old teddy bear, which made me think Our Guest had found the House of Mud spooky at night, too, but that didn't embarrass him. The one thing that seemed to bother the guy was a small, slightly worn book with a gray cover. My eye caught the name WAUGH, my old pal. (Not to be confused with WAR . . .) This reminded me of that miserable day Grandmother had told me I was like that no-good Phyllis Stine, whoever she was. The book didn't look like anything much, but it was causing Abercrombie to turn lobster red. He grabbed the book away from my sight line and nestled it inside the Navajo blanket. "*Really,* Ella . . . If you wouldn't mind . . .These are my *personal* effects."

He was pretty upset, but he couldn't say anything worse because the room filled up quickly with the two scuffling dogs, who always loved a kerfuffle, and the GM, who just said, "Good heavens! What's the matter? Have we found a rat?"

"Oh, Ella just *inadvertently* found her way into my suitcase," Abercrombie said through pressed lips, like I was the bad guy here. He snapped his case shut with a decisive *click* and I apologized again, but this time more for the GM's benefit.

There was a rat, of course, but the purple bathrobe and chili pepper lights were disguising him, and I had run out of time to do anything about it. The man was red as a guilty lobster, but I hadn't found what I was looking for. The Killer Dolphin. If he wanted to travel with chili pepper lights or some book by the famous Mr. Waugh, there wasn't much I could say about it.

When we went outside, the teenagers seemed to have sprung

up again, gathered under the cottonwoods to send Abercrombie off with some farewell text messaging or sunflower-seed spitting—however they expressed their affection.

Actually, that morning Tweedledum and Tweedledee weren't looking as pally as they had in earlier days. Jason and his uncle traded words, the way a catcher and a pitcher talk to each other on the mound with their mitts held up to stop people from lip reading, and then Abercrombie backed off and went into a smile-like-nothing-is-happening routine. More loudly, he delivered another one of his play-reading lines: "Well, make sure you get as much done in this last stretch as you can. We're counting on you!"—but he pretty well ignored Jackson.

And that was that. Tweedledum and Tweedledee were given the rest of the day off from the demanding digitizing magic, my grandmother and Darling Christopher exchanged an embrace, and Mr. Books managed a lip tightening in my direction that could, if you had a good imagination, be considered a smile. His white rental car vanished in the dust, and Violet Von Stern and I were alone again, with a couple of dogs and a hundred peacocks for company.

"Well, Ella!" she said. "That simplifies matters, doesn't it?" I had to agree. "Just the two of us ruling the roost again."

She started back to the house. "You leave soon, too, don't you?" she remarked. "Ten days." Not like I was counting or anything.

"It's always so quiet around here, and then suddenly, this summer—such a crowd." She paused. "Let's go to the Library, shall we? I could do with some encouraging."

How that big church of books would encourage her I couldn't say, but I tagged along. Sometimes, I've learned from watching Lou, tagging along gets you places.

"You spoke to your mother earlier, I believe?" the GM asked. "How is she?"

I was surprised Grandmother mentioned her: in all this time, she had kept references to my mom and her health crisis to a minimum. I thought of Mom's minuscule, scratchy voice on the phone, and my stomach clenched. I gave the GM my standard response, though: "Good." It was the easiest thing to say, and usually kept people from asking any more questions I didn't feel like answering. Besides, I wouldn't know how Mom was really doing until I saw her myself.

Grandmother pushed open the Librerery's heavy door, and we were greeted by the familiar smell of infinite words. She turned on the lights and surveyed the terrain.

"Did I ever tell you," my grandmother said, "about showing the Library to Amy?"

My mother? "No."

"Ah." She started walking up and down, gazing at books, taking out titles here and there as if to check on them. It was like Rosie or Carlos in the stables, saying hi to the horses, handing out Life Savers. These books were just as alive to the GM. "It was shortly after she and your father married. They came out for a visit."

I held my breath. I had seen their names written on my bedroom wall when I arrived, but the number of stories I had ever heard about my mom and dad when they were still together was practically zero. I always had a hard time remembering Amy and Walter Mackenzie had even been married. It just seemed so unlikely. The only good thing that ever came out of the disaster, it sometimes seemed, was me. If you considered me a good thing.

"I liked Amy, very much," the GM continued. She paused, holding a book called *My Family and Other Animals*. I liked that title. "I felt it was a shame when your father and she split up. Amy was amusing, and nicely mannered, and had a good brain. I kept skunks still, at that time . . . Have I told you about the skunks?"

Chanel Number 5 . . . "You mentioned them once," I said.

"They were charming. A much maligned species. Though having to de-gland them was quite a business. In any case. your mother was sweet with the skunks. Didn't bat an eye, just petted dear old Arpege as though he were a kitten."

That sounded like my mom. It was pretty hard to faze her.

"One day I offered to take her around the Library. Walter was rude about the place. 'Mother's mausoleum for dead authors,' he called it. He felt my collecting was a waste of money, and essentially frivolous. Unlike fishing, of course." Her voice soured; then she cleared her throat and carried on. "In any case, I'll never forget your mother, Ella. When she came into this room, her eyes grew wide and she said to me, 'Oh, Violet, it's like a chapel!'"

"That's what I thought, too."

My grandmother looked around the room, as if trying to see it. "Perhaps it is. In which case, Kepler's *Dream* was my prized relic." She sighed. "Your mother certainly understood the spirit of that book, Ella. I could see that."

Mom had handled the Killer Dolphin? This was news to me. "You showed it to her?" I asked.

"Well, not here," the GM answered, as if that were obvious. "No, no. By that time they were getting divorced. But right after I bought it, from Christopher. I made the mistake of returning via Washington. To see all of you."

All of us? Joan had told me about this before, but my brain still short-circuited, trying to imagine all of us in the same room. It was like a violation of natural laws. And my mom had never mentioned it.

"Your mother was properly reverent about Kepler's *Dream,* which I appreciated. I had just acquired the copy, and was terribly excited. Amy knew about Kepler from a different angle—she told us that his work with lenses and vision is still used to this day in the field of optics. This fascinated me. We had quite a conversation about Kepler together, before your father intruded with his"—her face darkened—*"disparagements."* I had the crazy idea that the GM herself had to delete an expletive there. "Of course, they were in the midst of separating, so there were fumes in the air. That acrid scent of divorce."

My grandmother did have a way of putting things. She was still gazing at her shelves, by now in a different patch altogether, in front of a line of slim green volumes. "Good heavens," she said suddenly. "Where on earth did this come from?" She took out a small book. "This has been missing for years. It's my old battered copy of *Hamlet*. I thought it had quite disappeared." She opened it, read for a moment and nodded. "Ah yes. 'One may smile, and smile, and be a villain . . .' Your father always liked that line."

"I spoke to him the other day, too," I told her. "Dad, I mean." I didn't see why I shouldn't tell my grandmother the guy had called. He was her son, last time I checked. "He was trying to tell me about July seventh in case I hadn't known."

"Yes. It was a terrible, unforgettable day, for all of us." Her voice was heavy. Then she frowned. "I beg your pardon. Did you say you spoke to your father?"

"Yeah—*yes*." I still slipped up sometimes with my language, especially when she sounded stern.

"Where was he?"

"I couldn't really hear. It was a bad connection. Some river, somewhere." I shrugged. "He was supposed to come here for a visit, you know," I told her sideways, as if I didn't think there was anything wrong with mentioning this.

She looked alert. "And would you have liked that, Ella?"

I nodded.

There was a silence. For once, Violet Von Stern didn't have any ready words at hand.

Luckily Joan, my movie godmother, made an appearance soon after this and offered to take Rosie and me off to the mall for some distraction. The three of us piled into her VW and went off to see some funny spy movie together in a big outdoor mall that could have been in Santa Rosa or anywhere. For an hour and a half I giggled like an idiot, drank soda, listened to Rosie smacking her gum and didn't have a single thought in my head about parents or grandparents or book thieves or cancer.

It was bliss.

Then, to top it all off, Miguel and Joan agreed to meet up at Casa de Estrellas, this cheerful outdoor Mexican restaurant with colorful lanterns hanging and that kind of peppy accordion music that makes you want to kick up your feet.

We ordered plates piled high with fajitas and *arroz con frijoles,* and Rosie and I were just retelling each other our favorite jokes from the movie when suddenly she looked up and her face jumped into bigger life.

"Uncle *Ignacio!*" she called, and before I knew it, we were surrounded by Miguel; Rosie's mom, Adela; and a shorter, lean man I didn't know, who all went into a warm group hug.

Joan and I watched from the gringo sidelines. When they pulled apart from one another Miguel explained that this was his big brother Ignacio, visiting from far away. Rosie's mom and dad were close—touching, not fighting!—and Miguel's face was lit as bright as I'd ever seen it, heart-of-the-fire bright, like the part that keeps the flames going. Ignacio was smaller than Miguel, with the same warm eyes but more lines around them, like dry creek beds running along the sides of his cheeks. He had weathered, darker skin that made him seem as though he had traveled to distant places and seen great, strange things. Both brothers had a quietness about them—I guess Carlos, in the middle, had to be noisier—but you could tell that Miguel was still in some kind of awe of his older brother.

Ignacio turned to me and did a double take. "You've got to be Walt's girl. Amazing. You're just like him!" His mouth cracked into an angled grin.

It was weird to suddenly be *Walt's girl* everywhere, when I hardly ever saw "Walt" in real life. And like I've said, around my mom, looking like Dad wasn't something I felt a hundred percent thrilled about. With the Aguilars at least it was a point in my favor.

"Ella, huh?" He shook his head, still with that wide, diagonal grin. "Your dad and me, we had some times together when we were kids."

"Yeah, they were the real pair," Miguel said as they all settled around the table. "Carlos and I were just the annoying little guys, tagging along."

"Well, Walt was nicer than me, more patient. He taught you how to bait a hook, anyways, Migo." Ignacio looked at Rosie and me. "And Carlos was good in the stables, even as a kid. Saddling up for your grandparents." He said a grateful yes to a beer Joan offered him. "How is your grandmother, Ella? She still ride?"

I shook my head, nearly choking on my *frijoles*. I still couldn't picture the GM on horseback.

"Violet is no horsewoman nowadays." Joan did a softer version of her car alarm laugh. "Airplanes and cruise ships are her preferred mode of travel."

"Things have changed at the hacienda, bro." Miguel sipped his beer. "Wait till you see it in the light. I was amazed when I first went there again after all this time." He stopped, as if wondering whether to go on, and Joan nodded to encourage him. "It's not the place it was. The animals are all gone; she got rid of 'em years ago. Now there are just a hundred peacocks, and souvenirs from her travels. And books of course. A million books."

Ignacio nodded. "Well, that makes sense. She and Dr. Mack both loved books."

"She had a whole library specially built after Edward died," Joan told him. "An amazing place. I tell her: 'Violet, a family of five could reside in there!' But no, it's just for her precious collection."

Ignacio listened with a distant look in his eyes. "Yeah, Dr. Mack and his books. It was your grandpa, Ella, who first got me excited about reading. And the stars, of course. *Las estrellas.*" He pointed at the restaurant's wall, where there was a dark, star-spackled mural tracing out shapes and signs of the zodiac. "The stars, and the human stargazers, too."

"Like Kepler?" Rosie asked pointedly. "Did he teach you about Kepler?"

Rosie's uncle tilted his head in a teacherish way. "Sure. Kepler was his hero." Ignacio traded a look with Miguel. "But also Copernicus, and Galileo. They aren't the only ones who made discoveries, though, you know. The Mayans knew all sorts of things about the constellations. They made remarkable astronomic discoveries of their own."

"Are you," I asked him shyly, "the uncle Rosie told me about who's been to Peru?"

He smiled. "Yeah, that's me. I'm the one." He stroked Rosie's hair with a gentle hand. "You girls should see what the heavens look like from *those* mountains."

He turned back to me. "Your grandpa, Ella—the stars were alive to that man. Dr. Mack enjoyed fishing, he and our *papí* had that in common, but he loved the stars even more. I sometimes think he loved them too much."

I asked him what he meant.

Ignacio sighed. "All I'm saying is, if he hadn't been so eager always to see the stars, he might have kept his eyes more on the ground." Seeing my confusion, he said, "I'm sorry, Ella. I'm talking about the accident. You know about that."

"Sure." I remembered what my grandmother had said, when she'd told me about it. "When they were all farther up on the Rio Grande, fishing, and my dad was being a daredevil, like usual. Messing around near the water. And then my grandfather had to jump in . . ."

"Well, no." Ignacio frowned and shook his head. "That's not how it happened."

"It isn't?"

"No, no." He waved a hand, as if to brush away the idea. "Walt was *asleep* when the whole thing started."

Ignacio looked around, as if wondering whether he should really go on. Miguel gave a silent nod.

"Our dads were out on the bank in the early, early morning,

drinking coffee they'd brewed on the campfire. Your grandpa—he wasn't a grandpa then, of course, he was just Dr. Mack, Walt's dad—was gazing up at the sky, like he did. It was probably four or five in the morning. You know how sometimes the best time to fish is before it's light out."

"'Catch the fish while they're still dreaming,'" I said, quoting my dad. "Before they're all the way awake."

Ignacio gave a sideways smile. "That's right. When any normal person is asleep in their bed, that's when you get fishermen out on the water, trying to fool the fish into swallowing a hook." Ignacio may have been smiling, but somehow it was the sadness lines that lit up on his face. "So Dr. Mack and Papí were getting ready to do some early a.m. fishing. I wanted to get Walt up, too—I figured we could see if our dads would let us join 'em. Dr. Mack was tilting his head back and talking about something in the night sky, as usual. Then he heard Walter's voice."

"Calling him?"

"No, not calling. Mumbling, talking in his sleep, I don't know what. Dr. Mack turned toward the sound and then he—stumbled over something in the darkness. And fell, backwards."

"Into the water?" I whispered.

"Into the water, over some rocks that slipped from under him. And then he got turned around, with it being so dark, so instead of climbing back toward the shore he went deeper, and the current was so strong it swept him in."

Ignacio took a deep breath. "And our *papí,* he dove right in after him and tried to pull him out. I was out on the bank, too, by then. I'd gotten out of my sleeping bag and was about to jump in, but my *papí* yelled at me to stay on shore, because the current was strong, and the water deeper than they'd realized—"

I knew how the story ended.

"And the Rio Grande," Miguel finished, "took both men."

The faces all around the table were somber. Beers were sipped. Rosie and I stared at the remains of rice and beans on our plates.

But meanwhile, an idea formed in my mind. "So does that mean the accident wasn't actually my dad's fault?"

"Your dad's? No, no." Ignacio shook his head, like a dog clearing its ears. "Walt was barely even awake yet. By the time he really woke up and stood next to me, it was over. Our dads were gone."

The creek beds around Ignacio's eyes were grooved deep with the old grief.

"Then why," I asked in a quiet voice, though I didn't know who I was even asking, "does my grandmother blame my dad?"

Joan reached across the table and held my hand. "It's like I told you once, hon," she said. "Everyone in a family has a different story about what's gone on."

"But she wasn't even there!" I protested.

"You're right," Joan said. "Who knows how she got that idea in her head? Maybe it was easier for her to think it was someone else's fault."

"Also," Ignacio added, "I think Walt did feel somehow responsible. Like he'd somehow made his dad fall, even though he didn't. He was a kid, we both were—just about the same age as you girls. He felt like if somehow he had acted different, or not been there at all, we might have had a different outcome."

"Plus, he didn't want his mom coming after Ignacio," Miguel said. "He didn't want any trouble of that kind."

"That's true, too." Ignacio looked at Miguel, and you could see years and stories move silently between the brothers. "The rest of our family hit the road pretty soon after that."

"And the road Ignacio took," Miguel said, trying to lighten the mood, I think, "turned out to be a lo-o-o-ng one."

Walter too, I thought: Spokane wasn't exactly around the corner. Neither was California.

It seemed like the GM had been so upset about Edward dying that she had convinced herself that his death was my dad's fault. That had to be one huge reason she had been a dragon to him ever since. A few other things came to my mind: the ashes in the Librerery fireplace, and the fighting phone call I had overheard, and a *Hamlet* book reappearing on the shelf. The pieces started to arrange themselves into an order that made sense.

"I know who took Kepler's *Dream*," I announced suddenly. A table full of people turned to me: Adela, Miguel, Ignacio, Rosie and Joan. In my mind had opened a clear space, full of light. Right at its center there was an image—of a penciled boy. "I have a feeling," I said, "that it was my dad."

Then, as if my words had been some kind of spell, conjuring him up from the restaurant's spicy air of pepper and pork and tortillas—there he was. Walking toward us.

My dad.

TEN

BIG
River

"Belle, old girl, how're you doing?"

My dad enclosed me in a monster hug. There were a lot of things that Walter Mackenzie was clueless about, but the guy did know how to give you a good hug. He was tall, big and brown bearded, and he wrapped his arms around you like a bear, making you feel safe and warm and only slightly suffocated. I hadn't had anyone much to hug that whole time, except Lou, who tended to squirm out of my hands after a quick slobbery kiss. The GM was a hand shaker, an eyebrow raiser—not a hugger.

So, though part of me was wondering why he hadn't *told* me he was coming there, finally, so I'd have known—or was that what all that CrxxxxZZxxx was about?—on the other hand: what can I say? I was glad to see him. He was still my dad.

After hugging me, he turned and shook Adela's hand, gave a big old back slap to Miguel—"Casa de Estrellas, here I am, like you told me to be, Migo," then leaned in and said to Ignacio, "Nacio, *Yo todavía no puedo creer que sea usted, hermano.*" My dad tried an awkward, I'm-not-so-good-with-kids wave to Rosie and introduced himself to Joan, who said in her honeyed voice, "I'm so glad to meet you, finally, Walter, I've heard so much about you," to which my dad replied, "Yeah, well, I hope not too much of it was from my mother." Everyone laughed.

It was kind of like a reunion. The grown-ups celebrated with more beers, and being kids, Rosie and I celebrated with sugar—doughnutty churros, hot and delicious. My dad settled down at the table with us, and I spent a moment just looking at him: that cute penciled face in the Haitian Room, all bearded and grown up.

"First things first," Dad said to me. "Ella, your mother sends her love."

"My *mother*?" This was bizarre. Since when was he a messenger for my mom?

"Well, yes," he answered. "You know, I've visited Amy in the hospital in Seattle when I could."

No, I hadn't known. Why did my dad always think I'd know everything if he never told me anything? And who could have guessed my dad would go see my mom? In my family, the words *mother* and *father* were never part of the same sentence.

"So. How is she doing?" My throat stuck on the question. I remembered her microscopic voice on the phone.

"Well, it's pretty brutal, what they do to people in these treatments." He shook his head. "They've put Amy through the wringer. But"—he looked me in the eye—"I think the disease is losing. It's running out of steam. Your mom's a tough opponent."

My heart skipped a beat. Everything else left my mind for a second except one loud, impossible hope. *Maybe she'll be OK.*

My business partner, though, was not distracted from the main question. "Mr. Mackenzie," she began, but when he said, "Walt, please, call me *Walt,* young lady," Rosie corrected herself. Shyly. "Um, Walt, excuse me, but I have to ask you: is Ella right? Did you take Kepler's *Dream*?"

I was impressed by Rosie's focus on the question of the stolen goods. Ms. Nelson had told us that focus was going to be important in middle school. Rosie would do fine.

"That (expletive deleted) book. Well, I didn't *take* it, exactly." My dad had the *it's not my fault* look I'd seen on him often enough before. He cleared his throat and turned to me. "Listen, Belle. None of this worked out quite how I'd planned."

Not a good start. This was what my dad had been saying to me practically since I was born. By now I could do a pretty good raised eyebrow, Von Stern style, so I gave it to him.

"My God, stop!" he spluttered. "You look just like Mother!" He raised his hands, as if in surrender. "All right, all right. Let's see. Where to begin exactly? So—I had been figuring out a time to come visit . . ."

"What happened," Miguel chipped in, "without your dad knowing it, was—"

My dad shook his head. "No, no, Migo—thanks, but I better do this. I should explain." He paused. The problem was, my dad wasn't really cut out for explaining himself. I guess when you spend all day fishing, you don't usually have to justify what you do. It's not like the fish are going to bug you about it. "Here's the story. There was a river expedition down the Colorado, and

I got a call from some old friends of mine who needed my help. Their regular guy broke his ankle and had to quit. It was around the time I had thought about coming here, to Albujerk— *Albuquerque*—to find out how you were doing, but these guys have helped me out in the past, so I said OK. I figured I could at least route the flight through here and see you, Belle, before I went to Colorado."

So he did think about me sometimes! I was flattered.

"But when I called Mother about coming in that night, she was not—*ahem!*—especially welcoming. She told me it would be"—he did a fake laugh—"let's see, what was that terrific word, *inconvenient* for me to come visit just then. Because she didn't have any kind of room ready for me, Dahling Christopher was ensconced in the Haitian cave, and you were in the John Hancock quarters." I liked that name, from the signatures on the wall in my room, I guess he meant. I'd have to add that to my house plan. "And all around the premises, by her account, were hardworking elves cataloging her (expletive deleted) collection of books . . . Sorry, girls." The apology was more for Rosie's sake. I was used to my dad and his expletives. "And so, short of stashing me up in the cottonwoods with the peacocks, she didn't see how she could fit me in."

"Oh, Violet." Joan shook her head. "You are naughty."

The Aguilars looked baffled, as if this story concerned a family of Martians.

"Yes. Mother and I had what you might call a *discussion* about it. The idea of being turned away because of Abercrombie, of all (expletive deleted) people . . ."

"The man is hard to like," Joan agreed.

"Hard to like? The guy's an—" My dad managed to stop himself, for once. "You know, my father didn't trust him. And then after he died, Dahling Christopher became very . . . *friendly* with Mother. He even proposed to her."

"What?" Joan and I squawked together. The idea was horrifying. Our Honored Pest would have been my . . . my step-Abercrombie!

"Thank God she had the sense to say no." He snorted. "I thought that would be the last we'd hear of him, that reptile, and he'd slither back down into his hole. Ashamed to have thought of himself any kind of equal to Edward Mackenzie. But no—he *persisted*. He tried to win her affections by giving her special book deals. He even sold her that volume she loves better than life itself. Kepler's *Dream*, I mean. So when I realized *he* of all people was the reason my own mother couldn't take me in—"

"You were a little annoyed," Joan suggested.

"Right. I was a little annoyed." He took a breath. "And I thought, what is she going to do if I show up, lock the (expletive deleted) doors?" Rosie's mom, Adela, kept wrinkling her nose, as if my dad's swearing were giving off an evil smell. He didn't notice. He was on a roll now, so he just barreled on, explaining that he got on his flight but it was delayed several hours, and he'd arrived late at night. He didn't want to wake everyone up, but he wasn't going to have made this whole Albujerk stopover just to sleep in some soulless Motel 6 either, as he put it. So, thinking what the *heck*? (he was really pleased with himself for a moment for cleaning up his speech), he decided to bed down in the *Librerery* for one night, in his sleeping bag. If it was good enough for Kepler and for Shakespeare, it was good enough for Walt Mackenzie. And then he'd see me first thing in the morning—Ella finally makes an appearance in the story, even if only as a passing reference!—with or without the Old Dragon's approval. He said he still had a set of keys, and the security code to the place—0-7-0-7—well, those four numbers were burned in his mind.

Ignacio and Miguel nodded at that. I guess that day, July seventh, was lousy for everyone.

Rosie kept pressing. "And Papí, did you go meet him then? Is that why I woke up and you were gone?"

Adela leaned forward. "No, Rosie, I called your dad. I had some news for him." She touched Miguel's arm.

"Oh." Rosie blushed. A kid, however tough, is always going to be glad if their fighting parents seem to like each other again.

"I generally take an evening walk around the property to make sure the place is secure; you know, every now and then we've had bulletins from the Juvenile Facility, not that anything's come of it. But that night, when I was out there, your mom called to tell me that this guy"—Miguel pointed at Ignacio—"had just arrived at the train station. Adela picked him up and brought him by," Miguel continued, "so I could lay eyes on him at least."

"They kept me in a running car out on the street," Ignacio

said, making a face. "As though I were some lowlife not allowed on the premises."

Rosie scolded her dad about not waking her up for that, but Miguel just shook his head and gave a look right back at his brother, explaining that they all agreed it wasn't a great time for Ignacio to run into Mrs. Von Stern again, after all these years. Not just yet.

"I didn't know any of this, either, by the way," said my dad. "I was just hunkered down in my mother's crazy, book-crammed *Librerery* at that point."

"Her 'mausoleum for dead authors'?" I asked him.

He grinned. "I did call it that once, didn't I? I seem to recall that ticked her off mightily." He shrugged. "It still seems like that to me. I guess that makes me a philistine. As she'd say."

"Who *is* Phyllis Stine, anyway?" I wondered, and my dad explained, with not too obnoxious a smile, that *philistine* is a word for a person who doesn't understand books and art. (Oh! Thanks a lot, Grandmother. Back at you: Would you know how to make a recipe out of a Roald Dahl book, if you had to?)

"Though I'm not as much of one as she thinks," Dad added. "There are some cool things in that *Librerery,* I admit. And I get a buzz seeing those pictures of my father with the astronauts. Especially Michael Collins."

"Mom always liked him best, too," I mentioned. "Mom and me both." I took a breath and kept going. I had to keep up with Rosie, here. "Anyway—while you were in the Library, let me guess. You built a fire."

"That's right." He didn't stop to ask how I knew. "I warmed up and gave myself a little light—it seemed better not to throw the bright overheads on—and then I thought, Well, what the (expletive deleted)? I might as well take a *look* at the Morris Kepler. Mother and I might have had a big blowout argument about that book years ago, when she first bought it—when it seemed like *that* was what she wanted to remember Edward by rather than, you know, her own son. Or, for that matter, her granddaughter." He looked at me again, more clearly. "But I remember, Ella, that your mom saw the point of the book. She thought it was beautiful."

"It *is* beautiful," I said. "It's almost like a kids' book, with those pictures. And the way he imagined life on the moon."

"That's right. And the Morris prints in Kepler's *Dream* are— (expletive deleted!)—they're amazing, the colors, the textures. That gold leaf. Not that I understand all the contents. If you want someone to explain the science of Kepler to you, ask that guy." My dad gestured to Ignacio, who shrugged modestly.

"It was funny—when we were kids, my dad loved telling Nacio all about astronomy, and his padre, Señor Aguilar, told me all the river lore about the Rio Grande. It was like us two boys traded places. On fishing trips, I learned all these great details about bait and casting, and Dad would spend hours tracing the constellations out for Nacio, here. So he was the one who ended up with his head full of stars."

"While you," I said to him, "ended up with your head full of fish."

I loved making my dad laugh: he had a deep, throaty chortle that made his beard shake. "That's right, Ella. Absolute. A head full of fish."

"So," Rosie prodded, "there you were, looking at Kepler's *Dream* . . ."

"OK, OK." My dad's focus wasn't as sharp as Rosie's. It was a good thing he wasn't going to middle school. "There I was. And in the firelight, that book seemed almost . . . *alive*." He lowered his voice. "This will sound strange, but I started to feel as though my dad—Edward Mackenzie—was nearby."

"There was something in the air that night," Miguel agreed. "Adela and I were aware of it, too. Almost from a different world."

A shiver found my spine and ran down it. Rosie scooched closer to me on the bench.

"Whatever it was, I didn't want to be in that (expletive deleted) mausoleum anymore. I decided I had to get out of there and check out the stars, like my father would have. I doused the fire—thoroughly, I've got camping tricks for that—and got my stuff together. But I held on to the book. It was almost like a talisman or something. A charm."

The Aguilar adults looked unsurprised, as though my dad were telling a story they had already heard, but Joan and Rosie and I were leaning forward in suspense.

"It was very cool to be out there in the starlight. Man, the stars were bright that night, so I just kept thinking about my father, and not the Old Dragon. I was wandering behind the house, where I used to run around and get into trouble as a kid, and then I found that familiar tree back there and—you know, almost before I had a chance to think about it, I just clambered onto the roof."

Ignacio started laughing. "We used to go up there together all the time when we were kids. Remember, Walt? Shoot BB guns from up there? Papí used to get so mad at us!"

"Yeah. I'm not sure the swans were too happy about it either." My dad laughed, too. "Though we never did hit any."

"Oh—" Ignacio had a mischievous kid grin. "We weren't really aiming at 'em."

"Hey, I think I saw you up there that night." Rosie was speaking to my dad. "That's one of the reasons I was scared. I saw a shadow near the tree when I went back to find Ella."

I remembered the thumping I'd heard overhead just as I was waking up. My dad was not a small guy. If there's a bear walking on the roof, you hear it—even if you think you're dreaming.

"I was kind of happy on the roof, you know, saying hello to all those crazy peacocks," he said, "but then I heard something that really gave me the chills. I heard this voice from a distance, and it sounded like—like *Ignacio*."

"I told you to be quiet." Miguel gave his brother a light punch on the arm.

"It seemed impossible," Dad said. "I hadn't seen Nacio since I was a *kid,* you know? As far as I knew, he was in Mexico or Peru or some (expletive deleted) place. I thought I was losing my mind. So I edged over near the front of the roof—"

"And I noticed something in the distance, on the roof. I

thought Walter was a ghost." Adela tsked at herself. "Or a robber."

Miguel nodded. "And so I went closer to the house, and fired a warning shot—"

"Not that that would have scared a ghost away," Adela added.

I was glad the grown-ups were amused—"It's like a scene from a comedy," said Joan—but they were forgetting something. Rosie and I were on the same track.

Me: OK, but so, Dad—

Rosie: What did you do with the *book*?

Me: —With Kepler's *Dream*?

Dad, *shouting, waving his big hands*: There wasn't time to think about the book! A shot was going off, and suddenly an alarm was yowling, and I just started to—

His big voice dropped suddenly, like it fell off a cliff. "To panic." There was a silence. "I'm sorry, Ella. The alarm, Ignacio's voice and then the *sirens*—it all brought back that early morning in July a long time ago."

"The sirens." Joan, who had mostly been quiet, sounded somber. "Of course. When the police finally found you boys by the river." Ignacio and my dad nodded. Ignacio took up the telling, saying that when my dad came down, they decided they had better get out of there and let Miguel handle things at the house. My dad would come back later to explain everything, and find the book and give it back.

He had hidden it in the cooler.

And *then* these two grown-up boys stayed up all night talking to each other, and as dawn broke, they went out to the cemetery together to pay their respects to their lost fathers. Before my dad knew it, his time was up and he had to get on the plane to Colorado to help out his buddies and see how the fish were biting. And by the time he had explained all this to Miguel, who went back to check out the cooler . . .

"The book was gone." Miguel shrugged. "Someone else must have found it. I looked all around there, you know, but it was gone."

Rosie and I looked at each other. *Abercrombie? Jason?*

The table was quiet.

After a few minutes Joan stood up and stretched and said she'd heard enough ghost stories for one night, and there were hungry fajita-eaters who deserved our spot. Arrangements were made in Spanish and in English, good-byes were said to Joan before she went off in her VW, and finally Miguel decided to let my dad drive his red truck back so Miguel could stay with Ignacio, Adela and Rosie—a flock of Aguilars. There were hugs good night all around, then my dad and I hit the road.

We didn't say much on the drive back to the GGCF. I think my dad was talked out, and I was listened out. Plus, we were probably both wondering how this reunion was going to go. He pulled in to the long canopied driveway, stirring up a cloud of peacocks. Grandmother's boat-car was there, and I could tell from the way he held on to the steering wheel for an extra minute that he was nervous. Finally we both got out of the truck and he stood, as if braced for a hurricane.

"Don't worry, Dad," I said. "Her bark is worse than her bite."

He looked at me skeptically as he hitched up his jeans. "Are you sure about that?" he asked. "As I recall, the Old Dragon has pretty sharp teeth."

He took a deep breath. "Mother?" he called out.

It was unusual for my grandmother not to come outside at the sound of cars arriving. I expected her in the doorway, Hildy in her arms, like the first day I met her.

But the only one who came to the screen door was Lou. We let him out, and he was full of licks and moans. Poor dog. No fajitas for him.

"Mother?" Dad called again. He made his way into the house, like an intrepid explorer. When he didn't come back right away, I started imagining he had found my grandmother and they were having a showdown, the way in cartoons the dog and cat end up in the same doghouse and you don't see the actual fighting, just the house bouncing around from the outside, sparks and exclamation points flying.

A few minutes later, though, my dad reappeared. No sparks, no exclamation points. He looked puzzled, but he didn't look beat up.

"She's not in there." He peered around, as if she might be hiding somewhere in the driveway. "The hacienda is the same crazy clutter as ever, though."

I thought about whether people ever kidnapped old ladies. Usually it was kids, right? They called it "kidnapping," not "ladynapping."

"Maybe she's in the Library?" I suggested. And so we made the familiar trek out by the brambles and the old skunks' pens, down toward the famous Von Stern *Librerery*.

Whose door was open. Hildy trotted out and seemed to nod at us, as if to say, *Yup—she's here*.

"Mother?" my dad tried again. Third time lucky.

"Walter . . . ?" came an answering voice. Dad didn't move right away, so I gave him an encouraging pat on the back that was maybe even a bit of a push. He went in, and I followed.

"Ah, there you are," Violet said to her son, exactly as though she hadn't kept him away from her house, or fought with him for a hundred years, or anything. "I wondered when you were coming."

She stood near a pile of books and papers, tall and straight as ever, but pale and drawn. My dad approached her carefully, the way you might a lion in its cage. But to my amazement, they embraced. I mean, it was more of the stiff GM kind than my dad's bear hug, but still—they weren't killing each other. That was something.

"I've just been out in the Library for a bit, thinking about Edward," she said in a faraway voice. "I was enjoying some of these old photographs again. I can't think why I don't have one here of you." That sentence hung in the air for a minute. Then she shook her head. "I know it's futile, but I thought I'd look one more time for Kepler's *Dream*. My lost relic."

My dad cleared his throat. "Mother, there is something I ought to tell you." Wow, I thought. Was he going to tell her right now? Talk about brave! "Some nights ago—"

"You were here," the GM interrupted. "Well, I knew that. You left me a souvenir. Thank you for returning my copy of *Hamlet*."

He nodded, and gave a half wave. "You're welcome." He tried again. He hitched his jeans up, for good luck. "But the other thing was—"

"You left a message on your father's grave. I saw it."

"Well, not a message, exactly," he said a bit sheepishly. I started wondering: how weird *were* these Mackenzies? What did my dad do, write a note?

"Those colorful fishing flies," she said, with a faint twitch of a smile.

"Well, they don't die, like flowers do." As if that were any kind of explanation. "I brought my father a few of my best. Ignacio and I went to the cemetery together."

My grandmother was startled. "Ignacio Aguilar is back in town?" She took that information in, and then gave her son a good, hard look. But her eyes were forgiving. "Well. I suppose everything comes full circle, doesn't it."

"Yes, and Grandmother," I blurted, "Ignacio told us about the accident by the river, and what really happened. And the thing is—"

My dad put up a hand to stop me. "There will be time to get to all that, Belle. But first, there's something else Mother and I have to talk about."

She nodded, as if in perfect agreement. "I told you that you couldn't stay here. Walter, I have realized that that was a mistake." My grandmother's voice did not falter. "More than that, it was an unkindness. For which I apologize."

This left my father speechless. I'm not sure he had ever in his life heard Violet Von Stern utter the word *apologize*. The rest of what he had to say vanished. He would have to get to it later.

"And I regret that I had Christopher staying here instead of you. I can see that that wasn't right."

It was as though these old arguments had caught up with my grandmother and almost knocked her over. She didn't seem completely steady on her feet. My dad actually held out his arm for her, and to my surprise, she took it. Together we all left the Librerery behind—for that day, at least.

"Don't worry about it now, Mother. Let's go inside."

Hildy and Lou were running around out there. Chasing the ghosts of skunks or swans, or whatever it was they did together.

"I should fix us some sort of supper. After all, here you are at last," the GM said as we walked back toward the house. I was filled to the gills with Mexican food, but Dad hadn't gotten around to eating at the restaurant. He'd been too busy talking.

"Well, I'd appreciate that," he said, "if you have the energy."

"We must have some cold meat in the refrigerator. And it wouldn't be hard to make some sort of slaw . . ."

Me and my dad—*ahem!* my dad and I—traded smiles behind my grandmother's back. The slawer, back in action!

And then the three of us went inside to sit around a table together in the House of Mud, for the first time—in history.

Dear Mom,

Only a week till I see you!
I can't wait!!!!!!
Abbie called—she's finally back from camp. She had a great time but was glad to get home. She said they made you fill out a sheet before you left saying "how you grew as a camper this summer" and she didn't know what to write. All she could think of was how her amount of STUFF grew. She had practically a whole suitcase full of all their craft projects: lanyards, tie-dye shirts, pine needle baskets.

I told her I hadn't done any craft projects at all, but have learned how to ride a horse. She was jealous. They don't have horses at her camp. Just kids, snakes and mosquitoes.

Anyway, Abbie said to say hi to you, and from her family, too. She asked how you were doing. I said they'd let you go outside and breathe real air again. We agreed that sounded good. Hospital air sucks.

We talked about all the stuff we're going to do in August together, swim and hang out and get ready for middle school. She asked about my hair and I told her it's in that awful awkward long/short phase still and it better look halfway decent by the time September rolls around or I am going to make you home-school me.

Talking to Abbie made me feel homesick for Santa Rosa for the first time in a while. I miss you all the time, but since you're not at home anyway, it's not exactly like I've wished I was there. And I've been having fun with Rosie, now that she is finally my friend. We're going to have a midnight feast before I go to Seattle. It's something she read about in a book.

I just went out to feed the peacocks. This is my last week for it. They're going to miss me when I'm gone. I think they're planning a surprise going-away party for me, but I'm pretending not to know. There will be Bobbing for Apple Cores, Pin the Tail on the Peacock and a piñata filled with corn kernels. It should be a lot of fun.

Most of what's left to tell you I may as well save till I see you. I hardly even have time to send this letter. Maybe I'll just come and drop it in your lap, like Lou does with tennis balls when he wants to play fetch.

I love you.

Ella

ELEVEN

THE
Plan

I HAVE ALREADY EXPLAINED THAT I'M NOT MUCH OF AN artist. Still, one of my goals as a camper this summer was to figure out how in the world my grandmother's old House of Mud was laid out. I had been working on a plan of the place for weeks now, and was pretty close to done. I wasn't sure what I would do with it when I had finished. Maybe enter it in next year's science fair. *House Plan: How One Old Adobe Home Can Be More Complicated Than an Ancient Labyrinth.*

I was sitting outside near the former pond (asteroid indentation), notebook on my knee, adding to my picture the constellation of cottonwoods the GM had told me about before. As I looked up to check on the pattern of the trees, I saw a hoodied figure approaching me. It was tall Jackson, without his sidekick.

"Hey," he said. "How's it going?"

Once again he was recognizing my existence! It was still surprising—like I had somehow managed in the past couple of weeks, in spite of not yet being twelve, to enter the ranks of the Visible.

"Not bad."

"What are you drawing?" he asked curiously.

"Oh, nothing." Which is the kind of dumb thing you say when you're nervous. It was pretty obvious I wasn't drawing nothing. "That is, my grandmother's house," I corrected myself, then showed him what I had so far. He looked at it pretty closely and nodded.

"You interested in architecture?"

Was I? I didn't know. "Maybe. I guess." Then, to sound less wishy-washy, I said, "Also, I think me finishing this might somehow help us find Kepler's *Dream*." I wasn't sure that was true, but it was a nice idea. As though, if we could just figure out all the nooks and crannies of my grandmother's crazy home, Rosie and I might have some breakthrough about what had happened to the famous *Dream* itself.

"Good luck with that." But the guy said this as though he meant it—not sarcastically. "*Somnium seu Astronomia Lunari.* The dream, or astronomy, of the moon. Right?"

I nodded. This surprised me: Jackson, at least, had taken in what the Kepler book was. He might have more furniture upstairs than my grandmother gave him credit for. A couple of chairs. Maybe even a sofa.

"Kepler got there first, you know?" he went on. "To the moon. In his mind, anyway."

"My grandfather thought he was ahead of his time."

"For sure he was. Though he caught a lot of flak for it." He pulled out a few sunflower seeds and started chewing them. I was wondering when we'd get to those. "That's why NASA named the mission after him. Because he imagined life somewhere other than on earth."

"Mission?" The word made me think of my mom. Her treatment being like a kind of mission. "Which one?"

"Their new unmanned mission—trying to find life, or the possibility of life, on other planets." He spat out a few shells. "It's this huge project. They call it the Kepler mission. After him. Same dude."

I was staring at him the way people do in a movie when a dog or cat starts speaking in a regular human voice. This wasn't what I expected to hear from the tall sunflower guy.

"Anyway, I'm getting out of here. I just came over to say goodbye. I'm going up tomorrow to Polaris." I must have still looked stunned, because he clarified, "The sci-fi convention, that is. Not the star itself. I don't have any space travel planned. Not yet." He gave a funny sideways look.

I laughed, hoping that wasn't uncool. "Yeah, me either." Again, not what you'd call a smart remark, but I was still more used to the mosquito treatment from these guys. I couldn't believe we were having an actual conversation.

"OK. Take it easy." Before he turned away, he added, "Hope you find it, by the way."

"Find what?"

"Your Polaris." He smiled in a hard-to-read way. "That is, you know—your dream."

I wasn't sure what he was talking about, so I just said, "Yeah. Thanks. See you later."

And he turned and walked away. I realized that Jackson was not, after all, someone whose back I was so eager to see. I returned to my drawing like I was super-interested in what I was doing, but in my mind I kept replaying what he and I had just said, and wondering through its meanings.

Beyond the cottonwood trees, in my plan, there was the place Miguel lived, and near there the feed bins, and I decided to add them, too. When I had begun this project, it was only going to be the house itself, but then I had to show the *Librerery*, and so I added some of the busted-up old coops, and decided the cabin and sheds ought to be in the picture also. I was just writing "Miguel's Cabin" in what passed for my best handwriting when something occurred to my sleepy memory.

That closed door.

The night Rosie took me into their cabin, when Miguel had disappeared and, as we now knew, my dad and several peacocks were thumping around on Grandmother's roof—well, I remembered that in that dim light I saw two other doors in the home Rosie and her dad shared. One must have led to the cabin's bathroom, but the other one to—what?

For the first time in this whole adventure I felt a flutter of a question about Miguel. If there was an extra room in there, what did he use it for?

"Hola."

A strawberry-scented bubble popped just about in my ear, and I jumped. It was Rosie, of course.

"Hi." I tried not to look startled.

"How's the map coming?" I showed it to her. "Looks pretty good" was her verdict, which was almost as good as getting a smiley face from Ms. Nelson. Then Rosie lowered her voice. "So—guess who knows the text-obsessed short kid?"

I shrugged.

"My cousin Lola." Rosie widened her eyes and waited for me to understand what a great lead this was. She popped another bubble. "*And . . .*," she went on, "Lola told me he's already gotten in trouble at school a couple times. Guess how?"

"I don't know."

"Hacking. He once hacked into the English teacher's grading account and gave himself an A!"

That seemed funny, the idea that Tweedledum would try to scheme his way into seeming smarter than he really was. "I guess my grandmother wouldn't have heard about that, though," I pointed out. "Abercrombie would have vouched for him. His nephew."

Rosie agreed.

"The other one just left," I told her. "Jackson. I think they're winding up their work today. He actually talked to me, about Kepler and stuff."

"Oh, yeah? Like he had any special knowledge of Kepler's *Dream*?"

I thought about it. "Maybe," I admitted. I realized you're not being a very good detective if you get distracted by the fact that one of your suspects is actually being nice to you. "He was friendly, anyway. That was new."

Rosie stood up, then put out her hand to pull me to standing. She thought we had better find the other one, Texty, before he went home, too. She still had a feeling that he was behind what had happened, and so did I.

We started to walk down the side path together, and I thought of that uncomfortable flutter I had had a few minutes before. I didn't want anything cluttering the air between Rosie and me, so I decided it was best just to ask her about that other room in her dad's cabin. I explained that I had wondered when it came to drawing it.

"Oh, the workshop. You want to see it?" she asked. "It's pretty cool." So we took a quick side-cut. As we stepped up the slatted wooden steps, I thought of the last time I had gone in there with this girl, who at the time thought I was something like an idiot (or at least a lousy rider). It's like I said before: friendship isn't a math equation. You never knew how things would work out.

As soon as we were inside, we heard a raspy sound coming from behind the closed door, and Rosie said, "I guess he's working." She stopped outside and knocked. When her dad opened the door, he looked surprised to see both of us but, to my relief, not annoyed.

"Hi, girls." He smiled at me. "Hey, perfect timing, Ella. I was just finishing this up for you. Come in."

And he ushered us into a small, sawdusty workshop that was completely crowded with tools and boards and sandpaper and aprons and oil . . .

And birds. On every shelf, bird after wooden bird. Small birds, big birds, seabirds, land birds, every kind of winged creature you could imagine. In a corner I even saw a peacock. I was pretty sure it was Carmen.

"Here she is," he said, wrapping his hands gently around a piece he clearly had just been working on. "She's a hawk," he explained. He offered it to me. "I made her for you."

Sure enough, there was a sharp-eyed hawk, standing with its wings folded, ready to fly if it needed to, probably looking for prey.

"For me?" I touched the bird cautiously, as if it were alive and might scare easily. It seemed magical: so smooth and soft, yet the surface somehow transformed into feathers.

"Your grandmother told me that was the name of your soccer team at home, the Hawks." He wiped a bit of sweat from his temple. "She doesn't much care for hawks, herself. But that's Mrs. Von Stern—strong likes and dislikes."

I had to agree with that.

"I gave your grandmother a dove once that she keeps in her room. After the real hawk got the other one." He put a hand on Rosie's shoulder. "And I made an eagle for this girl. Our name, Aguilar—you know, it's Spanish for 'eagle.'"

I gave Miguel a big hug. "Thank you. I mean . . ." I couldn't think of all the right words. He patted me on the back, like it was OK and I didn't need to say anything. I think we were both embarrassed.

Then he said I could take it now, he had just been finishing it. He wanted me to have it as a good-bye present, and for good luck. I was pretty sure I knew what he meant—about my mom.

I told Rosie to keep going on her quest for a last word with Texty, and she agreed. I had to find a safe place to keep my new pet bird, so I went back to my room.

By now, the path through the corridor and the Haitian Room and Tigger Hall was so familiar to me that I hardly saw the books and the bottles, the art and the armor. I had, finally, gotten used to my grandmother's many *things,* even if I could never in one lifetime know or understand what they all were or why she had them.

As Lou and I trotted down together into the John Hancock quarters, as my dad had called it, we saw an unfamiliar person in there, crouched down, reading the writing on the wall.

It was him.

"Belle!" He stood up to greet me. My dad was too big for the place, somehow. It wasn't the first time I had had that thought about him. Walter Mackenzie was one of those people who seemed naturally to fit better out-of-doors than in. "What have you got there?"

I showed him the hawk, and he whistled over it. "Miguel made this, right? Man, he does good work. Even as a kid, you know, he was always whittling stuff. That's beautiful."

I agreed, and then put the bird on the table by my bed. For this last week at least it could watch out for Lou and me, in the night.

"So, Dad, uh—" I pointed toward him, and the wall. "What are you doing?"

"Oh, I was just looking through the names," he said almost sheepishly.

"You and Mom are up there together," I said, as if he wouldn't know that already. Then, since I couldn't come up with a snappy phrase to capture the weirdness of that, as Violet Von Stern would have, I just made a googly face at him, a combo of *What the heck? Who'd have believed it?* with a small shade of *Why'd you two divorce, anyway?* mixed in.

It made him laugh. "Yeah, Belle. Well, parallel universes, you know? Parallel universes." His blue eyes—I saw them as Grandmother's eyes, too, now—wandered for a second. To a different universe, I guess. "In one of them, things go differently. My father lives."

I thought of something I'd had under my pillow all these weeks, the photo I had taken from the Chamber of Tchotchkes, of little Walter and a silvered Edward.

"Here." I took the small old square out from where I had hidden it, and handed it to him.

My dad took the picture from me, but didn't say anything as he looked at it. He was usually a pretty noisy guy, except when he was out fishing, but for a moment he was completely still. For the first time in my life I saw something that looked like moisture at the corner of his eyes.

Suddenly, there was a tapping at the back door and a strained whisper saying my name.

"Ella!"

My dad, startled, brushed his eye briefly with a thick thumb. "What the (expletive deleted)—?"

"That's Rosie," I said, though I didn't know why she was back there again, trying to get my attention.

"Ella," she whispered again. *"Come quick!"*

"Sounds like it's important." Dad went into the bathroom and to the back door. It was stuck, of course—as we knew.

"You can't open that one," I told him.

"This old thing?" he said. "Sure you can. There's just a trick to it."

He lifted his heavy booted foot and kicked the brass doorknob, hard. "You have to do that first." Then, cool as a cucumber (are all cucumbers cool? I mean, even if you don't keep them in the refrigerator?), he turned the knob, the door opened and there, just like before, was my new friend, Rosie.

She seemed as astonished as I was that we'd gotten through there, like we'd magically entered into the fourth dimension or something, but my dad, cheerful again now, just grinned. "This used to be my room, too, you know, Belle."

Well, no. It was one more thing I hadn't known.

We didn't pause now, though, as Rosie was urging me to follow her to the Library. She had been in there with Jason, she explained rapidly, to see him finishing up his work on the computer.

It turned out to be a good thing that I hadn't been with Rosie, because she was able to get Jason into conversation by making a passing snide comment about "the Royal Violet." (My friend was too polite to go into details about what she'd said.) She got the thumb dude chatting, turned away from his laptop, and then, she said, "I used my secret weapon."

I looked blank.

"Lola."

She could see I wasn't completely keeping up with her, but she let it pass. So apparently right on the spot she made up a whole tale about how her cousin Lola had been talking a lot about Jason lately. As Rosie said slyly, "It isn't a total lie . . . She did tell me about him."

Even Tweedledums and Tweedledees are open to flattery, we learned. Like I say, Rosie might have a future in drama, or at least in creative writing, because her master stroke was re-membering that Lola had gone to a pool party that day with some high school friends, and when she mentioned that, and how Lola had wondered if he would be there, Texty pulled out his phone and started going crazy with his thumbs, checking with someone else where this party was. By then Rosie was on a roll, so she emphasized that Lola was going to be there only for a little while, but if he headed over there fast, he might catch her.

Nice work, partner!

"But—now what?" I asked. I didn't feel too bad about tricking Texty, but I didn't see how it really helped us solve our case.

"Check the computer. That's the whole point. He left it on, and his file's still open. We've got to take a look."

So Rosie and I sat in front of the Tweedle machine, trying to make sense of what was in front of us. I'm sure I hoped Jason would simply have left us a message that said in block letters **"YOU'RE RIGHT, I TOOK KEPLER'S *DREAM*, I'M GUILTY GUILTY GUILTY!"** Unfortunately it wasn't quite that simple. The open file was a long list of author names and book titles. I wasn't sure what any of them would have to do with the Morris Kepler, but there was nothing to do other than read through, looking for clues. At first it just seemed one long, confusing blur, but I did notice that some names were highlighted. Rosie agreed that seemed significant. We just didn't know how.

The outer door creaked open.

"What are you girls *doing*?" came the alarmed voice of my grandmother, but right behind her was an echo from Mr. Cheerful, my dad, trying to reassure her.

There was a frozen moment of the GM looking at Rosie, and Rosie looking at the GM, and I think both of them were wondering if she was going to have a fit about Rosie being right there, in her priceless *Librerery*.

Here was where my dad earned his stripes, though. If he had stripes.

"It's Holmes and Watson, Mother," he said in his heartiest voice. "All Ella needs is a pipe. And one of those funny hats."

The GM took in a sharp breath, and I had a distinct feeling that she was swallowing a whole sentence or two, of the kind that might have made reference to our old friend Phyllis Stine, or maybe someone even less favored.

"Well, girls?" was all she said. "And what have you found?"

Now I had to hope we had something useful to show for our trespassing.

We showed the open file to my grandmother. You could see from the GM's grimace that the act of reading on the screen was distasteful to her, as if someone was getting her to swallow a nasty vitamin pill (like my mom used to make me do, in the mornings before I went to school). My grandmother agreed that what we were looking at was the inventory Tweedledum and Tweedledee had been working on all these weeks (I wasn't about to try to tell her their real names, not now). She did not know the significance of the highlighted sections either.

I noticed that one of them was Waugh. It was linked on the screen with something called *Decline and Fall*. I remembered the book I had seen in Our Pest's suitcase, that day he left when I had tried accidentally-on-purpose to rifle through his luggage. I told everyone about that, and about Abercrombie's eagerness to hide the copy from me.

"Really?" The GM looked interested. "And did you see what the book was?"

"Well," I told her, "he covered it up pretty quickly. But I did see W-A-U-G-H . . ."

"Waugh." She raised a brow. "You've always been a great fan of the Waughs, Ella, have you not?"

I gave it right back to her. "The greatest. You betcha."

My dad could see some joke flitting between his mother and me, and I could tell he was surprised. Impressed, even. It wasn't every near twelve-year-old who would risk sarcasm with Violet Von Stern.

My grandmother walked over to a particular patch of bookshelf where, it seemed, Waugh and his brothers hung out. She moved a finger along a series of spines, naming titles under her breath. When she got to the end of the line, she issued a single, distressed sound. (Not an expletive, as it would have been with my dad, but it was close.)

"Decline and Fall," she said wearily. "My first edition. A slightly foxed copy." She paused for an educational moment. "In book collecting, Ella, that means lightly worn." Then she faced all of us, her eyes a shocked water blue. Not icy. "My first edition is gone. It appears," her voice was somber, "that Christopher *is* a thief, after all."

From that point on, the four of us went back and forth between the highlights from the inventory Tweedledum and Tweedledee had created and the physical volumes on the shelves. Rosie or I would read out a name from the computer, like we were taking roll call, and Grandmother or my dad would compare the roll call with the volumes in her collection. Time after time we found that the boys were picking out the books of which she had doubles, and leaving those off their list.

The GM began to suspect that the "dire duo" didn't plan on their employer ever checking over their work. (Ms. Nelson would have had a word to say about that. She was very big on people checking things over.) "I'm sure they thought that I was old and doddering and not paying proper attention. The policeman that night, Barker, believed the same thing. What is more surprising"—my grandmother's voice became sharper—"is that Christopher himself was playing me for a fool. The way this list was being created, it is clear he was actively involved. He knew perfectly well which were the valuable volumes.

"Of course I have doubles: I have an early edition of *Room of One's Own,* but I also have one that is signed. The signed copy—Virginia Woolf's name, in her own wiry hand—is tremendously valuable. Christopher and I have talked about it, and I know he has coveted that copy. *It is not on their list.*"

I understood what my grandmother was getting at: Abercrombie had been trying, with the help of his nephew and Jackson, to erase the record of some of my grandmother's most important books. And when he had done that, I was pretty sure, he'd come back and handily collect those books for himself. As he already had with the Waugh.

"Christopher tried to persuade me—indeed, he *had* persuaded me—that he would grant me a magnanimous favor in coming to 'safeguard' the collection while I was next traveling." My grandmother gazed around the *Librerery*: her room, her church. "He planned to come with a moving truck, no doubt, and remove select treasures."

My dad reminded the GM that Edward had become wary of Christopher Abercrombie over the years, ever since the time Abercrombie sold him a precious volume that turned out to be a fake—something Grandmother said Mr. Books always denied he had known.

"Yes, but Father made Abercrombie take the book back and return the money." My dad looked at her. "He was not *terribly* pleased about that, as you may recall."

"No, he wasn't," my grandmother agreed. "But," she protested, "in other ways Christopher has been a good friend to me . . ."

"Friend?" My dad did a Class A eye roll. Really, worthy of a sixteen-year-old. "Mother, the man tried to marry you!"

My grandmother blushed. "Well . . . ," she said. It was one of the first times I'd ever seen her at a loss for words.

"And I don't think he was happy about your turning him down."

"He had bad feelings about Edward, too," I piped up. They both looked surprised that I had anything to contribute. "Abercrombie did. Rosie heard him talking about it. Remember?" Rosie nodded, and told them both the story of what she had overheard from the roof. My grandmother listened carefully and then sighed. Deeply.

"Well—perhaps this plotting on his part was a matter of settling old scores. Still, the insidiousness of the man! And the arrogance, thinking I'd never notice."

How the GM had managed to miss this before, I would never know. If I hadn't been a well-mannered young lady who tried, where possible, to be brave and good, I might have been tempted to say, *What did I tell you? The guy's a crook! He tried to make us mistrust Miguel. He said I galumphed. He probably secretly copied my words during Boggle games, too.*

"I remember when you bought Kepler's *Dream* from him." My

dad wasn't finished with Abercrombie yet. "I thought you ought to have the copy authenticated." Dad turned to define this for me and Rosie. "To make sure that it was the real thing."

"What I chiefly recall," replied the GM, some of the edge back in her voice, "was that you thought my purchase of that book was a waste of money and a complete folly."

"Yeah, well." He waved a hand. "Some of that was bluster. It was a lousy time, and . . ." His voice trailed off. Like I said, my dad wasn't great at explaining himself. "I hadn't been out on the river for a while. When I'm land-bound too long, it starts to show."

My grandmother nodded. "Edward needed his time on the river, too. That's a quality you shared."

"Is that him?" Rosie asked, pointing to the old photograph sticking out of my dad's shirt pocket. "Mr. Mackenzie?"

"Where did you get that?" my grandmother asked sharply.

"*I* found it," I said, guiltily. I wondered if I'd get in trouble for being a thief, too. "When I was looking around one day. Just, you know—exploring." I cleared my throat. "I just liked seeing a picture of Dad and his dad together. I—I was going to put it back before I left." I wasn't completely sure that this was true, but it seemed best to say so.

My grandmother looked at the small square for a long minute.

"Let's put this next to the others, shall we?" She walked over to place it, unframed though it was, on the shelf near the wedding snaps of herself with Edward. From the expression on her face I figured she wasn't going to give me a hard time, after all. In fact she suggested that my dad and Rosie and I could all go into that back room together (the GM didn't know to call it the Chamber of Tchotchkes) and look through the albums and loose photographs there, if we wanted to.

We did.

"You carry on then, Walter. Why don't you lead the way." Maybe, the GM said, we might even find some old snaps of the Aguilar boys running around in the dust from those days. Rosie's face brightened at that prospect.

Dad and Rosie went on ahead, but I hung back for a moment. There was a sadness pulling on the GM's shoulders that made me feel bad for her.

"Don't you want to see the pictures too, Grandmother?"

She didn't answer at first. It seemed as though her thoughts were miles, maybe even light-years, away. Finally she said, "That sounds very formal, Ella, doesn't it?"

"What? I mean—*pardon*?"

"'Grandmother,'" she clarified. "It sounds rather formal, don't you think?"

"I guess so." It seemed politest to agree with her, though since when had formality ever been a problem for this person who put you under house arrest if you didn't start the day with *Good morning*?

"Could we come up with something shorter for you to call me, do you think?"

"I don't know." By now I was used to sounding like I was in an old-fashioned play. It seemed late in the day to change the script, and besides, "Grandma" was still reserved for the name of my mom's mom, the brownie baker in Los Angeles. Even if she wasn't around anymore.

Then I thought of something. Taking my life in my hands, and trying not to sound nervous or mumbly, I said, "Well, how about—*GM*?" It was strange to utter the phrase aloud. That whole time I had only been hearing it in my head.

"GM?" She considered this as she opened the door for us back into the house. "Oh yes, I see. *GM*: Grand Mother. Or in German, Gross Mutter."

I wasn't going to touch that one. But I did add, "Or even, you know—General Major." Boy, had I become bold. Those elementary school teachers should see me now.

Violet Von Stern smiled her small, satisfied smirk. "Yes. Occasionally, for General Major. Well, someone has to keep things in shipshape, and it won't be the junior officers." She raised an eyebrow at me. "Though the junior officers do have their uses, of course."

She didn't put an arm around me—like I've said, physical affection wasn't my grandmother's style. But she did let me walk by her side, keeping pace with her as we made our way back to the house. It was a place where the junior officers were, in rare summers, permitted to be.

TWELVE

Dream
of the Moon

IT ISN'T A TOTAL DISASTER FOR A DETECTIVE AGENCY NOT TO be able to solve its very first case, but it's not great for future business. Someone must have opened up that old cooler and happened on Kepler's *Dream*, and it still seemed likely to the two partners of Aguilar and Mackenzie that short, speedy-thumbed Jason was the one. Then we figured he had come up with a way to spirit the copy to his uncle Christopher, to join the Waugh and who knew what else. How he could have managed to escape our eagle eyes—not to mention the peacock eyes around the property—was a mystery. That the Kepler book could never be sold would matter to any normal thief, but not to Abercrombie. He wanted that *Dream* for himself, I was sure of it.

But what could Rosie and I do about catching them? They had covered their tracks well, and the trail, after the excitement of the evil inventory intervention, had gone cold. Even with Lou on our side.

Anyway, time had pretty well run out. Up to that point, Time had been dragging its feet and hardly moving all summer, like a big fat horse stopping to eat weeds. Now suddenly, with the end in sight, Time moved into a gallop. It was a strange phenomenon, and if Kepler himself had still been alive, he probably would have had a theory about it. I figured if I ever became a scientist one day, I could make it a subject of my study: *The way Time speeds up and slows down again over a long, busy summer.*

For the past month and a half, all I'd wanted was to be able to visit my mom, but now that it was almost happening, I had butterflies in my stomach. It was surprising—I mean, this was *Mom* we were talking about!—but it felt like forever since I'd seen her. This was by a few light-years the longest time she and I had ever spent apart. Since I had never gone to wilderness or music camp, Broken Family Camp was my first serious stretch away from home. And though everything I had written to my mom about her being like an alien, or a clone, with her new blood, were just jokes . . . the fact was, I was worried. What if she really did look different, sound different? What if she didn't seem like herself?

Then there was me. I might have changed, too, and not just in the length of my hair. (Almost decent again, thank goodness, though it would need all of August to get to middle-school readiness.)

Sure, I'd been sending letters, and I guess Nurse Faye had read them out loud to Mom in the times when her eyesight or brain power were too weak to do it herself. But of course I left a lot out of what I wrote to her. I had to. There was only so much ground I could cover once a week, and besides, I had realized that sometimes you had to leave things out of the story you told, to keep things simpler.

It was especially hard to know what to tell my mom about my dad and my grandmother. When I was complaining about the GM, that seemed OK, because I never got the feeling my mom had been very fond of Violet Von Stern. But what if, by the end of my time at the GGCF, I actually, kind of, a little bit—*liked* my grandmother? What if I liked my dad?

Was that allowed?

For instance, I wondered if I would tell my mom about the nickname I gave grandmother, or finding that photograph of Edward and Walter, or for that matter any episodes that involved my dad. Mom had always hated the guy, after all. They were divorced—after all.

A situation Rosie, at least, was going to escape. It was pretty clear now that Miguel and Rosie's mom had changed their minds and weren't divorcing. In fact, Miguel was going to move back in with them at the end of the summer. He would keep working for Grandmother and mostly just use the cabin for his studio, to carve his birds.

Rosie was lucky: she was going to avoid the yo-yo, back-and-forth schedule and the nasty meetings in counselors' offices. We talked about it on my last night in Albuquerque, when she and I were getting ready to go stargaze.

We had wised up this time. No bare feet, no hypothermia: we had our dads' sleeping bags. If there is one thing you can count on Walter Mackenzie for, it's having a decent sleeping bag.

I think he was still surprised, even after a few days, to be in a real bed again. He told me he kept dreaming he was in Haiti, a place he'd never been, riding around on a motorbike in a strangely yellow light.

Rosie was the one who wanted to do a midnight feast up on the roof, as a way to say good-bye. I was surprised the GM let us, and she probably wouldn't have if I'd asked the wrong way. ("Me and Rosie want to . . ." or "Can we, like, go up on the roof?") But since I used good manners and the correct grammar, she said Fine. She even gave us two slices of cake, wrapped in tinfoil, as a kind of blessing.

It wasn't easy to get all our gear up there. I used the beat-up old cooler as a stepping stool, then handed things up, with Rosie hanging half off the edge like a bat and Lou running around excitedly below. In the end we had sandwiches, cake, oranges and a thermos of cocoa. We ate and drank bundled up in our sleeping bags, under the big, cold, black New Mexico sky.

The peacocks paced back and forth suspiciously, but kept their distance.

Once we were settled, munching sandwiches, we talked about the trail ride we had taken earlier that day. It was my last time at the Circle C, though Carlos told me I'd better come back because Paloma'd be waiting for me. Carlos had decided my butt was in good enough shape by now, as he put it, so Rosie and I went out on the mesa together with Lola and Carlos, keeping to a walk or trot to be safe. Even so, it was a thrill for me to be out in the scrubby, rust-colored landscape at last. I finally felt I'd earned those boots Abbie's mom had bought for me what felt like a thousand years before.

"You remember Kepler?" I asked Rosie.

"I know." She gave a sigh. "I can't believe we haven't nailed it—"

"No, not that Kepler." I was thinking of my first time at the Circle C. "The one I made up—that horse I was supposedly always riding back home in Santa Rosa?"

"Oh. Yeah." She laughed. "Wasn't he a 'pinto palomino'?"

"Yep. Pretty unusual horse." I could still feel the hard *smack* when I hit the ground that day. You have to get back on the horse, like everyone says, but the truth is, you never forget a bad fall. "Maybe I'll try to find somewhere to ride when I get home, though. It's not like there aren't plenty of horses in Santa Rosa. My dad said he might go with me, if he visits." The dim light helped hide the doubt on my face about my dad showing up. You never did know with him. Still, riding horses with my dad sounded good. It beat bowling.

Rosie and I stared up at the stars, wrapped up for warmth.

"You can see Orion really well tonight," Rosie said.

"Oh, yeah? All I know is the Big Dipper." It shouldn't have been true of the granddaughter of Edward Mackenzie, but it was. Some things, like star knowledge, aren't genetic: you have to acquire them all by yourself.

"Let me show you." So Rosie traced out for me the four outer stars of Orion, and then the three close together within, that were seen as his belt. "Orion's a hunter, you know," she told me.

"Some people call these three stars the Three Kings, or in Latin countries the Three Marys." Her uncle Ignacio had taught her all this stuff. Rosie showed me Orion, and then Castor and Pollux, and then how a couple of stars on the end of the Big Dipper pointed the way to the North Star, sometimes called Polaris.

This was my first real lesson in who was who up in the heavens. The North Star seemed like an especially good one to know. The one fixed brightness in the sky: once you found that, you would always be able to figure out where you were.

"This may sound weird," I told Rosie, "but that makes me think of my mom."

"Your mom?" She turned away from the stars for a minute. "How is she doing?"

"The story is she should be ready to go home in a couple of weeks. Though she's going to have to take it super-easy." Auntie Irene had promised she was going to teach me how to cook, because I would have to be my mom's main caretaker for a while. So far in life my main specialties were mac and cheese and cereal in a bowl. I was going to have to expand my range. "But they say it's looking like she could get better." *Could*: I didn't want to jinx it.

"What a relief," Rosie said. "My *abuelito* said she would. Remember?"

"Yeah." I took a sip from the thermos cup of hot chocolate, then handed it over to her. "You know," I told Rosie, "before we said good-bye, my mom told me it was possible she might die while she was in Seattle."

"Really?"

"Yeah." It was a relief to finally tell someone this. It had been one of those things I'd thought of, over these past weeks, anytime I couldn't sleep. "She said she didn't think it would happen, and anyway if she started to get a lot worse, they'd let me know and fly me out there right away. The flight takes three hours. She said, 'Even if I'm dying, I won't go *that* fast. I'll be polite and wait for you to get here.'" She had been trying to make a kind of joke about it, I realized later, but I wasn't laughing. I knew she must have been really scared, too—that was why she was trying to be light.

"What would happen if your mom died?" Rosie's voice was soft. "I mean—to you?"

"Yeah, I wondered about that." Nobody had a lot of confidence that my dad would suddenly pull himself together, I don't think. "I asked her."

The moment was burned into my memory, like a brand on the flank of a horse. Mom had been woozy and exhausted. It was one of our last days in Santa Rosa. There were all kinds of chemicals, not to mention cancer cells, running through her veins, and she really wasn't up for this heavy a conversation. Neither was I. But she must have felt she had to have it—maybe someone told her she should talk to me about death, since no one else had. There was a social worker named Grace at the hospital who sometimes tried to chat with me, but Grace found our situation tough. I think she had lines ready for husbands and wives and kids of people sick with cancer, but not one that included divorce. The divorce threw her off.

My mom didn't answer what I was truly asking her: *Who will look after me if you disappear?* I'm not sure she knew how to. So she went the cosmic route instead.

"She told me," I said to Rosie, "that I should think of her as going back to the stars. She said that's all we're made of anyway—that it's all the same stuff—" Stuff, Grandmother: Stuff! "You know, light and energy and matter." I looked up at the sky, trying to imagine that those sparkling tiny diamonds were really gigantic balls of fire and dust a million miles away. It still made my brain curdle to consider it. "And so, if she died, I wasn't supposed to feel too terrible, I was just supposed to look up at the stars and know that she was somehow back there with them, floating around in the galaxy."

We were both quiet a minute, looking up at the constellations, thinking it over.

"I'm not sure that would make me feel much better if it was my mom," Rosie said finally.

"No," I agreed. "It didn't make me feel better either."

This seemed a kind of depressing subject for a midnight feast. "Hey," I said to cheer us up, "you want some cake?" Cake is a great way to clear the air. I told Rosie that Grandmother's cakes were one of the things I'd miss when I was back home. And, in spite of the racket they made, the peacocks were another.

As if they heard me talking about them, a few of the birds

cried out, a high midnight cry, from the cottonwood trees in the distance.

"You know," I said, suddenly remembering what the GM had told me. "My grandfather planted those cottonwood trees in the pattern of the Big Dipper a long time ago. As a gift to my grandmother."

"That's cool." Rosie was impressed. "I still wish we could have known our grandfathers."

"Yeah. It's neat that you talk with yours, though," I said. "I've never heard a peep out of Edward."

We heard a scuffling, snurfling noise down below.

"What is that?" Rosie sat up, alarmed.

"Just Lou, snuffling around. *Lou?*" He gave a small, reassuring bark. "He's always finding stuff buried around here. He dug up some weird small skeleton a few days ago—I think it may have been one of my grandmother's old pet skunks."

"Pet *skunks*?"

"It's a long story."

Rosie rolled her eyes. *Those crazy Mackenzies.* She'd been hearing more stories from Ignacio about the old days, so nothing surprised her anymore.

Then her face changed. "You know what, Ella? If I accidentally found the 'stolen' Kepler's *Dream,* that's what I'd do."

"What?"

"Bury it."

"*Bury* it? Like a bone?"

"Yeah, you know—hide it somewhere." She sounded excited—like *she* had just dug up something interesting. "They knew they couldn't walk out of here carrying Kepler's *Dream*. So they found a place safe to keep it. Till they could come back, later." Her eyes were glittering. "Like when Mrs. Von Stern was away on vacation. *In Peru*."

There my grandmother would be, in the ruins of Machu Picchu, while at home . . .

"Though the problem is," she added, "then it could be *anywhere*. This is a big place."

She was right. Whenever I looked at my plan, I could see how much there was to it: the area by the Librerery; the whole back tangle; the scrubby bushes around Miguel's cabin; and the shed, near the cottonwood trees . . .

"Wait a second." The shed. The cottonwood trees.

I stood up, my sleeping bag falling down to my feet. "It wasn't Abercrombie. Or Jason."

"What do you mean?"

"It was *Jackson*!"

"Jackson?" Rosie was surprised. "But he's the only half-decent one."

"That's right. Maybe more than half." I thought of those odd, coded conversations he and I had had. "Jason should have just *chilled*": hadn't he said something like that? "They found the book in the cooler. But then they fought about it; Jackson didn't want to be part of some scheme with Jason and Abercrombie making off with the Killer Dolphin. So he hid it again. I think for him it was like a game."

"OK," Rosie said. "So what was the game? Where do we look?"

I remembered Jackson staring hard at the picture I had been drawing that afternoon. He wasn't just wondering whether I was interested in architecture.

"Polaris," I told Rosie. "He wanted me to find Polaris."

"What does that mean?"

"Come on!"

By now we were pretty good at clambering around in the pitch dark, so we got back down off the roof without breaking our necks. Lou had caught the spirit of the hunt—like I said, he had a good nose, and he could smell excitement in the air.

We made our way to the large, cratered area near the driveway. I showed Rosie as well as I could what I meant about the trees forming the Big Dipper. We looked up into their black and spooky limbs, inhabited by drowsy peacocks.

"Well, if this is the Big Dipper," Rosie said, making her own astronomical calculations, marking the line from one tree-star to another, "Polaris is over there. By the shed."

We both knew this area well. It was cluttered with feed bins, the odd shovel or hoe, random old junk. In any normal mood it wasn't a place where I'd have wanted to be fumbling around in the dark—there were snakes in Albuquerque, I was pretty sure, and I wasn't completely over thinking there were monsters, too, or ghosts—but by now I was so hot on the trail of the *Dream* that I stopped caring about anything else.

We went into the shed and clattered and clunked around the

old shelves for a few seconds, until my hand touched something padded and clothed. It felt human, almost.

I yelped.

"What?" Rosie came over and felt what I felt: a soft, cushioned wrapping around something large and rectangular that had to be . . .

A book.

We took it back out into the starlight. And there, almost glowing in our hands, was the *Somnium seu Astronomia Lunari,* Kepler's *Dream.* It had been wrapped up carefully, in a T-shirt that said POLARIS: FIND YOUR TRUE NORTH.

I thought of Jackson wishing me luck with our search and murmured, under my breath, "I hope he finds his, too." Rosie didn't pay attention. She was busy taking in the sight of this many-times-described object.

"Here, can I look?"

I realized that through all this time of hunting for Kepler's *Dream* my friend had never seen the book itself. She only had my word to go on that it was an important and luminous thing. So we opened it up, carefully, and paged through the moon, the demons, the vivid colors.

"Wow."

It was the same thing I'd said, I remembered. No wonder we made good partners. "It's incredible," Rosie breathed. "Like—a book of magic." Even in the middle of the night the gold shone. As if it were treasure.

Then we both got cold.

"Let's go inside," I said, and we made our way back toward the house.

The moment we opened the main door, we realized that light was coming from the kitchen and voices were talking together, low. This was a surprise. I would have thought the grown-ups would be safe in their beds, dreaming of Haiti, or maybe of Peru.

"You go, Ella—you show it to them," Rosie whispered. "I'm going back to my dad's cabin."

"No! Are you kidding?" I held her arm. "We've got to do this together."

"It's OK. It was through teamwork that we found it." My friend looked at me, and there was a warmth in her eyes that reminded me of Miguel. "But you know what? This is for your family. Your dad, and your grandma. Right now, it should just be you." She smiled, then gave me a quick hug. "Bye, Ella. I'll miss you. Good luck with your mom. Write me. 'Kay?"

"I will. I'll miss you, too." There was more to say, but I didn't want to start crying. That would put us right back at square one, where she was the tough one, and I had no grit. Rosie turned around and wandered down the dark path to join Miguel, who would be inside carving birds, or drinking hot chocolate, or maybe just staying up by the fire, ready to sit with his daughter and hear about our great success. I half wished I could join them.

But my job was to step out of the starlight and go inside my grandmother's house, where I would show her and my father Kepler's recovered Dream, or Astronomy, of the Moon.

Dear GM,

Well, I made it to Seattle. There are mountains here, too, but they're different from the Sandias. They're white, not pink, and look like the pictures you see on bottles of spring water.

My mom says to tell you hello. The hospital she's in here is fancier and more high-tech than the one in Santa Rosa. The doors make a sci-fi <u>swish</u> when they open and shut, and her germ-free room is ultra-clean. She has a view out of it, though, which she says helped her not go completely stir-crazy all those weeks. They are letting her outside now. I can wheel her out in the roof garden sometimes, which is a sign that things are going OK.

She said I ought to write a big thank-you to you for taking such good care of me while she had to be in here. So:

<u>Thank you!!</u>

Mom and I are going to work on a thank-you present for you, too, when she's a bit better. Maybe a coupon for a trip to Cape Canaveral or a chunk of moon rock or something.

Lou is very bored hanging around in our motel room. I bet he wishes he could play with Hildy. He sends his regards to you. (Though I never understood that: What does it mean to send a <u>regard</u>? Isn't a regard a look? How can you send someone a look, and why is that a good thing?)

I'm still working on my grammar and my language, as you see, so that should make you happy.

I hope your trip to Machu Picchu is amazing. Send us a postcard. My mom and I are planning to go there together one day. Maybe Rosie can come, too.

Please tell George hi, and no offense, but I think the Giants are going to shock everyone and win the World Series. That's just one girl's opinion.

I hope you're reading something good and enjoying a nice piece of cake.

Love,

Ella

POLARIS

I DID FIND HER AGAIN. SHE WAS RIGHT THERE, WHERE SHE was supposed to be. Just like Polaris.

I can't tell you how weird it was to walk in through the hospital doors in Seattle with my dad, going up to see my mom. I was nervous. I would have liked to have Lou with me, or more likely Auntie Irene, but this first reunion was a Mackenzie-only affair. Just the three of us. But if that combination had never made sense in the past, why should it start now? Some constellations of people just aren't meant to happen.

Still, at least Dad had been to the hospital before, so he knew his way around.

When the elevator stopped at the right floor, my heart started pounding. Nurse Faye came up to us, a small, round hen-like woman with an encouraging smile and a soothing voice I recognized from the telephone. She smiled at my dad and said to me, "Hello, Ella! I'm so glad to meet you at last," and gave me a warm hug, which was unexpected but made me feel a bit better. "Your mom is very excited to see you," she added. "Come on, her room is along here. You've sanitized your hands, right? The good news is you don't have to wear a mask anymore to go in." And she ushered us toward one of the many gleaming, huge silver doors along a bright corridor. "I want you to know your mom is an incredible fighter, Ella. She's inspired everyone here."

Swish, the door went as it opened, and in I walked to the place where my mom had spent six weeks in (mostly) Solitary Confinement while I had been falling off horses and getting back on them, eating cake and chasing imaginary thieves.

"Ella, sweetie!" Mom said. She was sitting up in bed wearing a thin toothpaste-colored gown I didn't recognize.

It was her.

I went over on shaky legs and put my arms around her for as long as either of us could stand it, and until I had finally stopped crying and laughing into her soft, familiar neck. In a way, that was easier at first than seeing her. She looked different from the picture I had in my head—worn out, like she had come back from a long, long journey—but as soon as I caught a glimpse of her face, or heard a snatch of her voice, I knew it would be all right. She wasn't an alien at all but still, in spite of the high-tech room, the disease and Aunt Miranda's blood, my mom.

She hadn't left me.

"Uh—" Dad said from the doorway after a few moments. "Amy? Ella? I'm going to leave you ladies together to catch up. I'll wait in the nurses' area, out front."

Mom thanked him with a wave and a tired smile.

If we were in a Disney movie, this would be the point where

the music would swell, the mom and dad might exchange sappy looks over the kid's head, and you would realize the parents might get back together after all, and the Mackenzies would re-form as one happy family again. After Making It Through a Tough Time. I think one or two of the nurses had that kind of scene in mind. And sometimes things do go that way in real life, even. Look at Rosie's parents.

My life wasn't a Disney movie. But that was OK, because it did have a happy ending.

The happy ending was that Mom got better.

"Look at you!" she said to me when we finally stopped holding each other and I stood by her bed where she could take in the whole picture of me, up and down. She was skinny as a rail, but her face was alive and full of light. "You've grown up so much, Ellerby! Horseback rider . . . Peacock feeder . . . Good grammarian. All these new skills you've acquired this summer while I've just been flat on my back here, doin' nothin'."

"Jewel Quest champion," I added. "Boggle pro. And detective—don't forget."

"I won't forget detective," she promised. "You have to tell me all about that. Oh! You're wearing the bracelet I gave you." She fingered the charms gently: star, heart, bunny. It had been around my wrist for the past six weeks, solid. She seemed pleased to see it.

"I have something for you, too, Mom," I told her.

And it was at this point that I gave her the present I had, all wrapped up in my favorite Hawks sweatshirt to protect it. I hadn't worn that sweatshirt all summer, once the GM told me how she felt about hawks, but this had seemed like a good use for it.

I helped her open it. Mom's hands were weak still—the treatment, she told me later, "wasn't just like getting run over by a truck, Ella, it was like getting run over by a jumbo jet—filled with overweight passengers"—and mine were clumsy with excitement, so it took a minute for us, together, to unravel the shirtsleeves and get at what was inside.

"OH!"

I don't know what she was expecting, but I doubt it was what she found herself holding: Grandmother's rare, Morris edition of Kepler's *Dream*. She stared at the beautiful, royal-blue cover, imprinted with the deep, golden globe of the moon.

"I remember this," she said softly in a low but happy croak, brushing her fingers over the blue. "I remember this amazing book."

She opened it slowly and leafed through the pages of artful script and vivid illustration. The diagrams of the planets. The descriptions of lunar life.

"It's for you, Mom," I told her. "It's yours now."

"What—?" Mom looked at me, her thin face pale with amazement. "But—how did you find it? And how—how could Violet ever give it up?"

"It's from all of us," I clarified. "Grandmother. And—Dad. And—*me*."

This information made her speechless: not from weakness,

but from shock. Finally, my mom put the book down on her bed for a moment and held my hand tightly. She looked into my face and around my half-grown hair with serious eyes, like she had an announcement to make. Then she said in a cracked voice, "I should have kept up with Violet over these years, Ella. I'm sorry. She's your grandmother. It shouldn't have had to come to—this"—she gestured around at her room—"for you to meet her."

I held my mom's hand. "It's OK," I said. I didn't want her to feel bad, and anyway, I was thinking, if I'd had to hang out with Violet Von Stern before I was eleven years old, she might have scared me so much, I'd have had to hide under the bed.

"Now, tell me. Tell me what happened to Kepler's *Dream*."

So I told her how it all happened. How Dad took the book, and then how Jackson found it, and how Rosie and I had figured that out finally . . . as well as what Abercrombie had been up to, scheming with his nephew.

"But—" My mom gazed at a jeweled blue page that held images of bright stars against deep, black space. "Why is it coming . . . to me?"

This part was harder to explain, in a paragraph or two, with complete sentence structure and correct punctuation. You really had to be there, at the House of Mud, on the day I left, in a cluttered, dog-loud kitchen that had three generations of Mackenzie in it, even if one of them had turned herself back, after her husband's death, into a Von Stern.

All I could say was that the look on my grandmother's face that morning, when I came into the kitchen, was from another world. It seemed as though she and Dad had already been up for hours together. They were both early birds. It was one of the things they had in common.

"Walter and I have been talking for some time, Ella," she began. "About many things—but also about this book, and what it has meant to me over the years. How it represented your grandfather. As I explained to you, it felt in some way like a token of Edward."

I nodded.

"And your father said something that I think was—*correct.*" She and my dad traded some sort of eyebrow moment together. I bet he hadn't heard *that* sentence very often. Not from his mother, anyway. "He said that there are other, less material ways I can remember Edward that may be more important. Why, every time I look up at those cottonwoods planted in the star pattern, I think of him."

I wasn't sure where she was going with this. But I tried to look awake.

"And so, your father had the idea"—she *ahemmed,* for good measure—"that by all rights Kepler's *Dream* should be—yours."

Mine?

"Mine?" I squeaked.

Lou barked, Hildy yapped and the GM said, "Hush, Brunhilda!" sternly.

Dad just said, "Yup, Belle, old girl. This book properly belongs to you."

"But—" I couldn't help hearing Abercrombie Books's voice in

my ear. *Good heavens, Violet—you don't let the child handle it, do you?* I was only eleven! I wasn't a grown-up yet. The thing was worth a lot of money! (Expletive deleted)!

The idea made my head pound. I thought of everything I had heard about this book: what it meant to Grandmother, how rare it was, my dad holding it in the middle of the night and feeling the spirit of his own dad, and the scene my grandmother had described to me from years before, when she had shown the book to her son's soon-to-be ex-wife, Amy Mackenzie.

And there was only thing I could think of to say.

"Can I—can I take it to my mom?"

Grandmother looked at me with eyes I recognized: eyes that reminded me, strangely, of that very person—my mother. It was pride in there, I was pretty sure. A bright blue pride.

She stood up, gave me one of her stiff, tall lady hugs, and said, "Of course you can, Ella. That seems entirely the right thing to do. Of course."

And then, before all the emotion in the air made everyone too uncomfortable, my dad started making noises about getting to the airport, and the GM reminded me that I had to sign the wall before I left. So I went back there and did it, with glitter pen so no one could miss it:

ELLA MACKENZIE. And then, because it wasn't the whole story without him, I added AND LOU.

After that, the morning turned into a blur of departure. My dad and I said a final good-bye to Grandmother, who by that point was holding Hildy close to her again, for company. I thought I saw a tiny sparkle in the corner of her eyes—it might have been diamonds, or then again it might have been something else—but then the GM started scolding me for how sloppy I looked, and how she really hoped I'd brush my hair before I went in to visit my mother after all this time, even if the hair itself hadn't yet declared its allegiance to the side of the short or the long, and before I knew it, we were bouncing out of the driveway in Miguel's truck, dust and feathers flying, as he drove us to the Albuquerque Sunport so we could get to Seattle.

"And so," I concluded, as I told this whole story to my mother, in her super-clean hospital room the day of our reunion, "this book is what you get for completing your mission. It's like the presidential Medal of Honor they gave to Michael Collins. And the other guys, too, of course—Neil and Buzz." I felt weirdly shy now. Around my own mom! So I kept up my patter. "In a perfect world I would have liked to organize you a ticker-tape parade, but that was a little hard to plan, staying at Grandmother's."

"I can see that." Mom nodded. "The logistics would be difficult. Especially if you couldn't get online—you'd really need the Internet for that kind of thing."

That was her kind of joke. Yup—she was definitely still Amy Mackenzie. She might be thin and faded, like a mom who has been through the washing machine too many cycles, but every day she became a little better and a little stronger. Her colors got more vivid. After we were settled back in Santa Rosa, remaking life at home again, her hair started to grow back. It wasn't the same as before—the blond had turned a sort of ash gray, and it was weirdly frizzy—but, as she said to me, "Hair is hair, Ella. I'll take it."

She has had the host disease problem from time to time, the one Auntie Irene warned me about. Random outbreaks of illness, when the new blood fights back against the old stuff, or maybe it's vice versa, but Dr. Lanner has been able to calm down the worst of their arguments and get Mom better again when it happens. And with Ella Mackenzie as head chef, whipping up gourmet meals of roast chicken and lasagna, the patient improved rapidly. Eventually Mom was even able to pet the dog again, and Lou was good enough not to hold the long hands-free, high-hygiene period against her.

I hardly ever talk to my dad about the House of Mud, or what happened that summer. When he and I get together, which still isn't all that often, we talk about other stuff . . . *Ahem!* I mean, things. The ups and downs of river life, or middle school. How incredible it was when the Giants won the World Series. He did give me an astronomy book that describes the constellations, and I tell him that in between soccer and homework and everything else, I sometimes curl up in a corner and read parts of it. I doubt I'll ever be an expert, like Edward was, but I'd like to get as good as Rosie in knowing who's who up in the heavens.

It goes the other way, too: the GM and I, when we're on the phone, don't talk much about Walter. She has other people to gossip to me about, like Miguel and Adela (and their new baby!), or Joan (who got engaged to someone at the bookstore), or even George the UPS guy. Every now and then the GM throws in a sly line about Darling Christopher—and it is *not* usually complimentary. Grandmother was grateful to me for getting her to go to Peru. She told me that Machu Picchu was "extraordinary" and that my mother and I will have to go. One day we will.

Mom takes very good care of her copy of Kepler's *Dream*. Sometimes we'll look at it together when my hands are nice and clean, leafing carefully through the stories and diagrams, the pictures of the planets. Mom and I agree that we don't know what the (expletive deleted) Kepler was talking about exactly in his wild *Dream,* but we like how bold he was back then in imagining travel to the moon one day. How the guy tried to see hundreds of years ahead of his own time to other improbable things that would happen, too. "That takes vision, Ella, to imagine the future," Mom told me once. "It takes genius."

And when we're finished looking at it, she puts the book back in its safe, sheltered place on a high shelf in her bedroom. My mother agrees with something Violet Von Stern once said, that an object so treasured shouldn't be locked away completely where people can't enjoy it. But she wants to keep it protected, too: to remind her of everything that happened that summer, to both of us, and to have something gold and beautiful near her while she dreams.

ACKNOWLEDGMENTS

Behind this novel stand a great cast and crew, to whom I owe many thanks:

Story consultants Ann Packer and Ann Cummins, who read early and often; Peggy Orenstein, Mary Pols, Kate Moses, and Carol Edgarian; executive producers Linda Brownrigg and Nicholas Brownrigg, who had assistance from Philip Lewis and Valerie Brownrigg; location scouts Michael Brownrigg, and Victor and Peter Engel; ghostwriter Sylvia Brownrigg; legal counsel Barry Williams and Paul Barulich; development advisers Anna Webber, the late Pat Kavanagh and Rosemary Canter.

Gift baskets are owed to my wonderful, ever-encouraging US agent Geri Thoma and tirelessly dedicated editor Stacey Barney, both of whose suggestions, responses and guidance have improved this book tremendously, from its first rough cut to this final print.

I am also honored by the graceful visual shape given to my story by the gifted team of Annie Ericsson, Chris Sheban, and Irene Vandervoort.

Special gratitude to my in-house market tester Samuel, who saw the dailies, and Romilly, my focus group; and to Henry, who once had to be brave, and good.

My deepest appreciation goes to the London office, Sedge Thomson, whose loving support throughout this production has been generous, enduring and crucial.

Over the whole of *Kepler's Dream* has presided the spirit of my grandmother, Mrs. Harry Batten, the original and incomparable GM.

And her peacocks.